What could go so

THE SEDUCTION OF MOLLY O'FLAHERTY

wrong?

SIERRA SIMONE

Cover Design by Natasha Snow

Cover Image by Ebru Sidar / Trevillion Images

Edits by Evident Ink

CONTENT WARNING

The main character in this book has experienced sexual assault in the past and experiences it again in Chapter Four of *The Persuasion of Molly O'Flaherty*. The past assault is remembered in Chapter Eight.

While Chapters Four and Eight can be skipped and their events inferred from the following chapters, the assaults are referenced throughout.

PART I: THE SEDUCTION OF MOLLY O'FLAHERTY

CHAPTER 1

*T*he front door closed with a slam, and I finally allowed myself to dissolve into tears.

How had I let it come to this? Me, the girl who used to fight the dock boys in Liverpool, the girl who had not once but twice faced down the bull in my uncle's pen back in Ireland?

It wasn't enough that I'd been slowly goaded into this trap by the board of the shipping company I'd inherited from my father. But I'd also given the leader of the board, that *troll* of a man, the ability to make me cry. That itself was worse than the way he'd forced himself on me. If I could have endured it stoically, maybe I wouldn't mind.

Well, I would mind still. But then at least it wouldn't poison my dignity as well as my body.

I used my skirt to scrub at my tongue and the insides of my cheeks, ignoring the tears running down my face, which turned instantly cold against my skin in the chilly room.

I cried even harder as I remembered for the ten thousandth time that I had no options. I'd never known a woman to success-

3

fully report a man taking advantage of her when the man was as wealthy and powerful as the leader of my company's board. Especially with my...unconventional...reputation, I worried it would be all too easy for Mr. Cunningham to convince a court of law that my testimony was not to be trusted. And I couldn't fight back in any other way, verbally or physically, or he would see to it that I lost my company.

And I couldn't talk to anybody about it. By now I'd kept the secret of Cunningham's shadow over my life for so long that I didn't know how to un-keep it. Just imagining the look on Helene's face or Adela's...and how could I tell any of the men and not have them look differently at me? Like I was Molly O'Flaherty, a victim, instead of Molly O'Flaherty, a red-headed, fiery-tempered heiress?

Besides, I wasn't sure that Julian or Silas wouldn't kill him, and I didn't need that complication right now.

No, I would just have to endure. As I had since I was fourteen.

I had practically rubbed the inside of my mouth raw, but I still couldn't un-taste what had been forced in there, and now my mouth simply tasted like silk as well as the bitter taste of Cunningham, and what was the point? He'd defiled me before and he would again, and I had no choice if I wanted to keep my company. That's just the way it was.

I slid off my chair onto the freezing floor, finally giving in to the deep urge to actually sob, which I did. I pressed my cheek to the cold wood and cried and cried, my whole body shaking, my breathing so fast and shallow that I felt dizzy and light-headed and I didn't care. I *wanted* to pass out, I *wanted* unconsciousness, because when I was unconscious, this didn't exist. It wasn't real.

The only real things were dreams of steely ocean waves and rocky beaches and a dark-haired man I knew so well...

A dark-haired man I'd been avoiding.

And it was not the man everybody thought I was in love

with. It was someone else. Someone I knew just as well. Someone with blue eyes and an easy grin and a big—

There was a knock at the door and I stiffened, knowing my butler would be there to answer it, which meant he would walk past the front parlor, where I was currently a puddle of rumpled silk and tears. I sat up, wiping furiously at my eyes but unable to stop the actual crying, and then the horrible thought struck me that it might be Cunningham, back for more, and he would see me crying and know how much power he had over me. I gulped in a huge breath and forced myself to hold it, scrubbing at my face with my dress and trying to stand up, and then the front door opened, even though the butler was nowhere in sight, and someone stepped through and I kept holding my breath, *be strong be strong be strong*—

Silas Cecil-Coke stepped into the hallway, casually shucking his woolen coat and draping it over his arm, and he was humming under his breath as he turned and saw me. *Silas.* My heart split open with relief and also with so much shame, that he of all people should see me like this, that he of all people should bear witness to my weakness. My breath left my body in a jagged exhale and with it went my self-control; my tears returned with triple the force and I buried my face in my hands, desperate to hide all this messiness from him. All my messiness.

"Molly?" I heard him ask, voice laced with concern and surprise. Quick footsteps, and then I felt him drop to his knees next to me, his hands in their cold gloves pulling at mine.

"Sweetheart. Look at me," he murmured.

I couldn't stop crying, so I just shook my head, the small movement making me dizzy again, because I couldn't get enough air and I didn't even want to try to get enough air. What was the point?

He gently peeled back my hands and then the cool leather of his gloves pressed against my flushed cheeks and my feverish forehead. "Darling Molly," he whispered. "My Molly. What is it?"

His words were too tender and too kind, the starkest possible contrast to what Cunningham had just done to me, and some foolish part of my mind hissed that I didn't deserve his lovely words, that if he knew what I'd just done, then he'd drop his hands in disgust and walk away. I sobbed even harder at this thought, the truth of it curling tendrils around me, into me, into my very soul.

You don't deserve him. And either way, he wouldn't want you if he found out...

"No, darling, I didn't mean to make you cry harder," Silas shushed, gathering me close. My face was pressed against the clean-smelling fabric of his morning jacket, my body cradled between his hard thighs, and he began to rock me back and forth. "You can tell me, lovely. Whatever it is, you can tell me."

I shook my head again, the finely spun wool of his clothes abrading my cheeks as I did. I couldn't tell Silas. I mean, I couldn't tell anyone, but especially not him. Not after this last summer when I'd realized that the strange tightness in my chest whenever I thought of him, my preference for him and him alone when our friends played together, the surprising loss of the jealousy I'd felt toward Ivy Leavold—now Ivy Markham—when all these years, I'd assumed I was in love with Julian.

It had all come to head when Silas and I had fucked on Julian's parlor floor after introducing Ivy to our version of Blindman's Bluff. I'd wanted to use him to show everybody that I didn't care about Ivy, that I didn't care about the obvious attachment Jules felt toward her, but in the middle of it all, I'd looked down at Silas, at his adoring blue eyes and his dimpled smile and wide shoulders, and it finally started to make sense. Somehow along the way, somewhere in our decade of friendship, I'd fallen in love with Silas. And I had no way to process that revelation; I'd thought that I'd loved Julian—in fact, *everyone* thought that. But what I felt for Silas was so much deeper, so much subtler, so much sweeter, and it scared me. I'd never felt that way about anyone before, *ever*.

6

I'd done my absolute best to avoid him ever since that moment.

But of course, he was here now, seeing me at my most pathetic, and there was no way to undo the damage this moment was doing. Even if he never found out about Cunningham, he would still walk away from this thinking I was weak and womanish, the kind of enervated female who sobbed and fainted at the slightest provocation.

In fact, any moment now, he would let go of me and wish me a good day, and leave, grateful to get away from my chaotic emotions. I was sure of it.

He didn't.

Instead, his arms moved around me and then I was lifted into his arms as he rose easily to his feet. His lips swept across my forehead in a chaste gesture that was so unusual for him, but so very Silas at the same time, and then he carried me upstairs, into the blue and gold sanctuary of my room, laying me on my bed. My tears started to slow somewhat as he bent down and rekindled the banked fire in the fireplace. A good fuck might make me feel better...

I started to sit up to pull off my dress, and then Silas stood up and saw me. "No, love," he said. "I'm going to take care of you. You lay back and stay still, and I'm going to make you feel better." His voice was sweet and attentive, but there was something deeper in it that I'd never heard before, something about the words maybe, or something about the intensity in his gaze.

Whatever it was, my body responded immediately. I lay back down and waited patiently, my tears still flowing, but quieter now, softer. Everything had a blurry sheen to it, blurry and slowed-down somehow, as if time had begun to run differently. I watched as he took off his jacket and unknotted his tie, and then tossed both into a nearby chair. His shirt collar hung open now, exposing the strong cords of his neck, the delectable curve of his Adam's apple. He walked over to the bed and started unlacing my boots, and watching his long fingers easily manipulate the laces was so inexplicably erotic, or maybe it was the way he glanced up at me when I shifted on the bed, a stern glance as if he suspected I was about to disobey his request for me to stay still. Whatever it was, it pulled heat from my face down into my chest, deeper into my stomach, as he pulled off my shoes. As he wrung out a damp, cool cloth and began to sponge the tears off my face.

I looked up at him, at those eyes with their sweeping eyelashes, at those slightly parted lips, at those cheekbones seemingly cut from stone, and he met my stare with a sweet smile, and it was too much, this intimacy without sex, this closeness and care without agenda. I looked away, my cheeks burning.

Could he tell, I wondered, what strange, complicated feelings he inspired in me? Could he read everything in my eyes? Did he know that for the last six months, I could only come when I thought of him, did he know that I indulged in long, embarrassing fantasies about a future that could never exist?

And if he did know, could he ever feel the same way?

His fingers wrapped around my chin and rolled my face back to his. I resisted a little, but the motion was insistent, and when my eyes met his eyes, the combination of the authority and devotion there took my breath away. The cloth moved over my lips, dabbing gently, and it was as if he *knew*, knew that my mouth was the one place I needed to be cleaned right now, but also the place that his touch burned the worst, because having this man that I loved touch the place where Cunningham—

I tried to turn my face away again, but then he bent over me and replaced the cloth with his lips.

"Don't move," he whispered against my mouth. "Just let me have it."

Oh God.

His kiss tasted like Silas—a clean, fresh taste with a hint of gin. And it felt so classically masculine—firm and warm and not too soft, determined and restrained all at once. I breathed in the breath that he breathed out, his parted lips just barely pressed to mine. No tongue, no motion, and normally if a man had his lips against mine, I'd take charge. I'd reach up and find his neck with my hand, and then I'd flip us over so that I was on top, driving the scene. But he'd immobilized me with nothing more than the firm authority in his tone and the blueness of his eyes, and so I stayed frozen as he brushed his lips against my mouth and then began nibbling on my jaw and throat, his hand sliding underneath my neck to tilt my head up and give him better access to what he wanted.

And that's exactly what it felt like, like he was taking what he wanted—kisses and bites and licks, as if he'd laid me out here simply to taste my skin and sample the hollows of my throat and upper lip. I'd never let men take what they wanted from me; *I* was the one who took what she wanted, but for some reason, this didn't bother me right now. It didn't bother me that someone looking in from the outside might claim that Silas saying those words, *just let me have it*, was as degrading and violent as what Mr. Cunningham had done, because I knew it was different. For a thousand reasons: that I wanted this, that Silas cared for me, that we had ten years of trust bricked between us.

And somehow, *somehow*, this was what I needed. Because everything terrible about the day faded away, all the despair about my future fading away too, and there was just the bed so soft under me and Silas with his cufflinked wrists cradling my head and the tight warmth building low in my belly.

My body relaxed, and my breathing finally slowed to normal. Silas's lips moved with a languorous pace, lapping up my remaining tears and kissing my hair and licking the inside of my mouth, pulling away whenever I tried to kiss back, which made me relax even more. I didn't have to think, didn't have to decide, didn't have to be in charge. For once I could simply lie back and *feel*. Hands moved under my back, lifting me up to tug at the laces that cinched my dress closed, and again he whispered,

"Don't move," this time with his lips pressed to the front of my throat.

I didn't move. Even when the dress was tugged off my shoulders, even when the skirt and petticoats vanished too, and my stockings were all that was left. After his work was done, he stood up and unfastened his cufflinks, tossing them carelessly onto the end-table, his eyes on my body like somebody appraising a bottle of wine or an elaborately prepared dessert. The appreciation of a connoisseur, objectifying and glorifying me all at once.

I managed to stay still as he rolled up his sleeves and unbuttoned his shirt, as he came onto the bed and straddled my shoulders, pinning me down as he slowly opened up his pants, exposing the long jut of his cock, already hard, already swollen. I dropped my eyes to it, hungry for it, and then there it was, pushing without apology past my lips and into my mouth. For the second time today, I had a cock in my mouth, but this time could not have been more different. Silas's murmured words, *be my little doll* and *suck harder* and *your mouth is so good, Molly, so fucking good*, made me wet and squirmy, and his hands threading into my hair made me feel like a princess, and his dick was the most perfect thing I'd ever tasted—nothing about it felt wrong or shameful or violating. In fact, I embraced the similarities; every stroke of Silas's cock erased each stroke of Cunningham's, every dirty word Silas whispered erased the humiliating ones Cunningham had spoken. And where Cunningham had been clumsy and uncaring, Silas was deliberate and careful. He wasn't thrusting into my mouth, he wasn't stroking fast and hard against my tongue—he held my head and moved in slowly and thoroughly and rhythmically, almost like he was doing it for me and not for him.

"There," he said. "Isn't that better? Isn't it all better with my dick in your mouth?"

I nodded, looking up at him and then moaning at his face, so uncharacteristically assured and commanding, that normally smiling mouth pressed into a line of masterful determination. He reached down and ran his thumb along my lower lip, which was stretched wide to accommodate his girth, the first hint of frenzy glinting in his eyes. "Such a pretty mouth," he muttered, speeding up the rocking of his hips. "Such a pretty face. Such a pretty girl."

I flattened my tongue against the underside of his cock, tightening my lips around him. He hissed out a sharp breath. "My pretty girl."

Yes, *his* pretty girl, I wanted nothing more in that moment than to be his girl, his Molly, because somehow I knew that Silas would make it all go away. Maybe not forever, but sometimes, most of the time, because he would shelter me when I needed it, bring me to a bed and remind me that there was a place where my only responsibility was being *his*.

In fact, just that thought, just the word *his*, sent so much heat to my cunt that I had to rub my thighs together, but the moment I did, he pulled back, his cock sliding from my mouth with a wet pop. "You don't think I'm going to take care of you?" he asked, his voice somewhere between cold and demanding. I searched for a glimpse of his usual joking self, his usual ready grin, but it was nowhere to be found, and a small thrill chased down my spine.

"I—"

"I told you not to move. Because I'm going to make you feel better." He raised his eyebrows. "Don't you trust me?"

Now that my mouth was free, now that we weren't touching —save for his knees against my arms and the slight pressure of his ass against my stomach (it didn't escape me that he was careful to keep his full weight off my body)—now that things had slowed down, I could think again. And that was a bad thing, because all of those bad thoughts had returned, telling me I was contaminated, that Silas wouldn't want me if he knew what had just happened, and so I opened my mouth to tell him, to explain.

"Silas, I do trust you. But before, when I was—" my voice

cracked, still raw. His hand stroked through my hair, soothing me, and his eyes were deep wells of affection and concern. Despite the dark wet cock still arcing between us, he was totally still and completely attuned to me. I licked my lips and swallowed my pride and tried to forge ahead. "When I was crying…"

My voice faltered again. I couldn't finish. I wasn't ready to tell this story yet, even though Silas was ready to listen. And then I felt even more embarrassed, even more ashamed. I couldn't even whisper the words. How weak was that?

Silas looked down at me, his expression thoughtful. And then he pressed his fingers against my lips. "Not yet. You don't tell me yet."

I blinked up at him, confused, because I *couldn't* tell him, I couldn't say it, and that was the problem. And then those strong fingers pressed against me even harder, and I realized what he was doing. He was lifting the failure from me by taking away the choice, he was erasing the moment of weakness by telling me I wasn't allowed to succeed anyway.

"Whoever made you cry—they don't get to be here right now," he continued, his eyes boring into mine. "Not even in your mind. Right now, you are the most important person in this room, and the only thoughts I want you to think are about your pussy and your mouth and your perfect tits. Understood?"

I should have been irritated at that—normally, I didn't like being told what to do with my own thoughts. But this time, he'd rescued me from the inescapable pit within my own thoughts, and I couldn't have been more grateful. His words soothed me and calmed me, and I closed my mouth, catching the tip of his middle finger between my teeth as I did.

He growled and leaned down over me, settling on his forearms and pressing his body against mine. "I asked you a question," he said and ground his bare cock against my clit. The direct pressure after so long without stimulation…I groaned, trying to lift my hips up to him. He raised up just high enough so that my endeavor was pointless, the tip of his cock bobbing down onto my belly. I could feel the drop of pre-cum he left there and I shivered.

"I asked you a question," he repeated, reaching over to tug on one erect nipple. "I want you to answer me. Do you understand?"

He tweaked the nipple—hard—and I whined. "Yes," I whimpered. "I understand."

"Good girl." And then his cock was back, steel-hard and hot against the sensitive flesh of my cunt. "Now be my little doll and stay still."

I did, catching my breath as he slid down my body, kissing his way to my navel and then farther down, to the top of my silky copper curls. He glanced up at me, as if to make sure I was obeying and staying still, and then he braced his hands against my inner thighs and spread me wide. But he didn't dip his face down to my cunt, not yet. Instead he seemed to be drinking the sight of it in, the sight of me spread open for his pleasure. And part of me wondered if Silas and I had ever done this before; if I wanted to be licked, I generally sat on his face, as I did with all of my lovers. I didn't like laying back and having a man's head between my legs, and I knew exactly the reason why I didn't—

No.

I wasn't letting Cunningham in. I would listen to Silas and only think about myself. About the breath tickling against my clit as Silas slowly lowered his mouth, about the jolt of electricity I felt as his tongue slid against my folds for the first time. About the curling fingers of tension in my pelvis, weaving a tight, hot knot there, *right there*. I finally dared a glance down my belly, and what I saw nearly made me come right then and there. His fierce blue eyes trained on me, his hands on my thighs, his whole mouth moving on me, jaw and lips and tongue, like I was a fruit he was trying to devour. And we kept our eyes locked the entire time, even as he guided two long fingers into me, pressing against that perfect spot, even as his other hand snaked over my hips and stomach to hold me still against the bed. And it was those blue eyes—eyes I'd looked into a thousand times but never like this, never with him in control and so *focused*—it was those eyes that shepherded me past my lingering shame, past everything, into one of the strongest orgasms I'd had in years.

Pulses spread from his fingers and his mouth, powerful pulses that curled in and crashed on themselves, waves rippling outward from my core to my chest and legs, and finally to my fingers and my toes. The waves were relentless, never-ending, wiping away all thought and all feeling and all memory, because there was nothing left but eyes, *blue eyes*, and that flat, hot tongue and the small cries I couldn't stop from issuing from my throat. And then Silas was over me, one hand braced next to my head, the other at the base of his cock, the tip rubbing me from clit to ass, ass to clit and then it was notched in place, the crown just barely inside my hole.

"Whose little doll are you?" Silas asked.

"Yours," I whispered, still downright malarial from my incredible orgasm. "Only yours."

"And who takes care of you?"

"You do."

He nudged in a little deeper, so I could feel exactly how much he stretched me. "And what are you going to do right now?"

"Not move." I moaned as he slid in farther. "Let you make me feel good."

"Good girl." Silas dropped a kiss onto my lips and then pushed in all the way, giving me a moment to adjust as he did. And then he began making love to me. Not fucking—this wasn't fucking. Despite his edict that I needed to lay still, despite the way he leaned down and growled those delicious words again —*stay still, just let me have it*—there was something different here than there usually was between us. I could see it in his eyes, in the way his stomach muscles tensed as he moved with complete control and restraint. Normally, when we fucked, we were friendly and affectionate, but we were both there for our own pleasure.

But today, Silas was only here for *my* pleasure. Or maybe even that wasn't quite right, because this was about more than pleasure right now. He was healing me, caring for me, in a way that no one ever had before, and somehow he could sense this, I thought, sense that this was some sort of watershed moment for me.

And as his head dropped to nuzzle into my neck, I wondered if it was a watershed for him too.

In the spell of his touch, I'd forgotten that I hated this position. I hated not being in control of the depth and pace, and I even more hated not being in control of my own orgasms. But all that was cast aside right now, as if the Molly that felt all those things was lying in the same discarded heap as my clothes, and I was a new Molly altogether, one who gasped and then sighed as Silas shifted so that the hard muscles above his dick ground against my clit as he moved.

"Your pussy is so sweet," he breathed in my ear. He found my hands with his, lacing our fingers together and bringing my hands up over my head. His body was stretched along mine completely now, the sides of his white shirt brushing against the place where my skin met the bed-sheets and the fabric of his trousers chafing the insides of my thighs. And now he had the whole weight of his body on me, pressing me down into the bed as he drove his dick into me, deep and hard and angled just right, and I should hate it, I should hate having a man's weight on me, but now he was kissing me so perfectly, with such demanding vigor, and I never wanted it to end, having the man I loved on top of me, kissing and penetrating, everything wet and warm and still raw from my earlier tears.

And suddenly I wanted him to know that. I wanted him to know that I loved him, that I wanted him and only him, but before I could break our kiss to say the words, my second orgasm rolled home, an abrupt cliff I hadn't expected but leapt off happily, squirming under him as his cock and the friction of his groin against my clit drove the orgasm over the edge and sent me tumbling into oblivion. I cried out as the first contractions took me, clenching my cunt and my belly, and then there was sensation everywhere, heat and joy and fluttering, passing through me and leaving numbness and tingling in their wake. I couldn't feel my fingers and toes, and the first thing that greeted me as I slowly came back was feeling of Silas's mouth hungry on mine, as if he wanted to eat my sounds, as if he wanted to taste my soul.

And I wanted to taste his. I wanted to taste his everything—thoughts and feelings and pain and pleasure and everything that made Silas himself, I wanted it all. For the rest of my life. And I couldn't stop myself, not with the lingering waves of joy—coming so soon after those miserable, lonely waves of pain—not with his perfect mouth against mine and his perfect cock still worshipping me.

"I love you," I murmured when he lifted his head, and then time stopped.

Silas froze, his jaw clenched, his eyes pinned on mine, the words echoing in the room despite how quietly they were uttered.

I love you I love you I love you...

He didn't speak for a moment, his face painted in an expression of impassive withdrawal, and even his hips had halted, his cock buried up to the root.

I made a mistake, I panicked. I'd said the wrong thing, let go of the wrong secret, and now I'd ruined what had been the best moment of my life so far, and *why* had I said that?

Except then he cried out, low and long, his head dropping to my shoulder and his body trembling over me as he pulsed hot and fast, pulsing so hard that I could feel his warmth surging into me. His hands squeezed mine as he drove his hips even deeper, his breath stuttering and shuddering against my collarbone, and I could feel every moment of his climax, every throb of his cock and every beat of his heart and every jet of cum, until he finally let out a long exhale and relaxed, his hands releasing mine and finding my face and my neck, his mouth hot against my ear.

"I love you too," he breathed, and then before I could answer, he was kissing me again. His cock, which had never softened, was now moving inside me again and there was no time to worry about what I'd said, about what he'd said. There was only time to feel and to come, again and again and again…

PART II: THE PERSUASION OF MOLLY O'FLAHERTY

PROLOGUE

*N*ot many men sail to France with a black eye. But then again, not many men fight with Molly O'Flaherty and live to tell the tale.

I leaned against the deck, smoking a cigarette and watching the waves roll past the ferry, churning and frothing against the sides. I could go down to the saloon and enjoy a glass of port before we reached our destination, but even though the journey from Dover to Calais was short, I didn't much fancy the idea of spending it with inebriated strangers gawking at my black eye.

No, better to be alone in the dark, where I could lick my wounds in peace.

The problem was that I knew exactly where things had gone wrong. I knew where I'd crossed the line from occasionally fucking Molly O'Flaherty to falling in love with her. And that line had appeared when I'd found her sobbing in her parlor on Monday morning, tears glinting off her cheeks, her red hair lit like fire by the winter sunlight.

She was so achingly beautiful and so achingly alone, my stubborn Molly. And the moment I thought the word *my*, as in *My Molly*, it had hit me with hurricane force.

I loved her.

And in the matter of three short days, I'd managed to fuck it up so irreparably that there was no other choice but for me to leave the country. I would probably never see her again.

And after what I'd done, that was the best thing for her.

I flicked the cigarette into the cold, choppy water and went down to the saloon to get drunk after all.

CHAPTER 1

SILAS

EIGHT MONTHS LATER

"*A*re you really sure you want to go?" my brother Thomas asked.

We were outside the Provençal villa Thomas and his wife Charlotte had rented for the year—a year that was likely to turn into two, given Thomas's general state of contentment and Charlotte's swelling belly. They were working on the sixth Cecil-Coke baby, little usurpers I liked to call them. Each one held a spot between me and inheriting Coke Manor, and I reminded them periodically of this—like right now, when I had little Henry pinned to the ground and was tickling his sides mercilessly.

"Yes, I'm sure," I told Thomas over Henry's squealing laughter, and then I bent down and pretended to eat his chubby little cheeks. "I won't stop until you promise I can live with you when I'm old," I warned my nephew.

"I promise! I promise!" Henry squawked.

And then—*ambush*. Arms around my neck, arms around my waist. Soon I had four Cecil-Coke tots wrestling me to the ground, and I was subsequently vanquished, my hair pulled and my pockets robbed of the penny sweets I kept there for just such instances of raiding.

"I'm defeated," I declared, flopping over dramatically onto the dry, sweet-smelling grass. "I've been destroyed. By tiny monsters."

Giggling, the children scampered off. I sat up, smiling, and dusted off my clothes.

Thomas regarded me from his chair, where the fifth Cecil-Coke was snoring soundly against his chest. "Then again, I think I see now why you're so eager to set off." His voice was dry, but he was mostly joking—we both knew how much I adored my little usurpers.

"It will be better this way," I said. "I'll go and handle the family business in London, so you can stay here in your lavender-scented bower."

Thomas thought I was leaving to act as his proxy in some legal affairs across the Channel—which technically wasn't *un*true. I *was* planning on doing those things. But he didn't know about the letter from Julian Markham in my breast pocket, a letter I'd unfolded and refolded and unfolded again countless times over the past two days.

A letter about Molly.

"I hope I can come back before Charlotte has the child," I said, standing up. "The tiny, squinty, sleepy part is my favorite."

The four older children burst out of the back parlor and onto the patio, running past us straight into the gardens, making for the vast lavender fields below. They were jostling, arguing, and laughing, and my chest twisted.

"Actually, I think every part is my favorite," I said, and my words weren't joking or light-hearted. They were heavy with longing. I wanted this—*this*, with the happy screams and the constant noise around the dinner table, and the way Thomas and Charlotte looked at each other like there was no other person they wanted more in the world. The way they gathered together by the fire on chilly nights, the way Thomas and Charlotte always woke up with piles of children in bed, no matter where all the children were put the night before.

I wanted a *family*. I'd wanted one for some time. And fuck, if that wasn't unsettling. Because people in my circle didn't want families. They wanted freedom and money and infinite amounts of leisure time bled free of responsibility. I used to want those things too.

I'd been corrupted. Corrupted so thoroughly that I was in danger of becoming a good person. But I also wasn't an idiot. I knew I'd never have what Thomas and Charlotte had; there was no way I was capable of that kind of selfless, pure love. I'd proved that to myself—and everybody else—eight months ago.

But maybe, just maybe, fate was giving me a chance at something else.

Thomas was watching me as I thought, his thick eyebrows pulled together. "You know, it's time you thought about starting a family of your own."

I gave him a weak smile. "I'll think about it."

"I'm serious, Silas. You slept your way through England, and then you slept your way through half the Continent, and now you've slept your way through le Midi. And you don't look any happier for it, at least not since you came here. Surely you can find a nice English girl that will make you content?"

"You know me," I said, getting ready to leave, "one English girl alone would never keep me satisfied."

But an Irish one might.

The thought came out of nowhere, unbidden and unwelcome, and I banished it immediately. If there's one thing I've tried to carve into my soul these last eight months, it's that:

I.
Was.
Not.
In love.
With Molly O'Flaherty.

∼

IT TOOK a couple of days to get to London, a couple of bright, windy days with the July sun burning into my skin until the Channel ferry could take me back to the sceptered isle. I reread Julian's letter as I boarded the Dover-London train, skipping past all the usual letter-writing pleasantries to the only part I could think about.

...As for Molly, well, I don't know if you've heard, but the word is that her company's board has finally unveiled their plan for making her heel to their whims, something they've been trying to maneuver for years. They've declared that they will leave the company and sell their shares to the next-largest competitor if she does not marry within six months. Moreover, they want this man to be someone they personally approve of.

Naturally, this has sent every wealthy and connected dolt to London in order to woo both the company board and her. One can only imagine how furious and lonely this has made Molly...

I stopped reading, folded the letter back up, and leaned back in my seat, pinching the bridge of my nose.

Molly was in trouble. And not just any kind of trouble, but the kind where she was being forced to marry. Even though I didn't love her, not one bit, *not at all*, the thought of her standing in a church with any man other than me dug a knife into my chest. It was easier leaving her last year, if any part of it could be called easy, when I'd imagined she would remain unattached and alone forever. That if I couldn't have her, then at least no one else would either.

So this mass audition of potential husbands was, in the words of Edward Rochester, a blow.

A very strong blow. To my naked heart. With a blunt instrument.

Which was, of course, how any friend would feel about any other friend being caught in a web of misfortune. It didn't mean anything special that I suddenly couldn't think about anyone other than Molly. It didn't mean anything special that I hadn't been able to sleep the night I had read Julian's letter, that I had tossed and turned in my bed, tormented by the memory of sky-blue eyes glittering with pain.

I should go to London, I'd realized that night, staring at my brother's French ceiling. *I should use this chance.* To help her and to help myself with one single, golden opportunity.

And maybe, in the process, set things right between us. The only problem with that being that I had been the one to set things so very, very wrong in the first place.

Molly and I had known each other for years—almost a decade—and we'd kissed and fucked and frolicked like mad across Europe and back into England...no different than anyone else in our group. But then Julian had gone and fallen in love, and something had changed for all of us. I couldn't describe it properly, not even to myself. I just knew that it was some sort of malaise, some kind of apathy, and that what used to be fun and playful had suddenly grown dull. Was there a limit to how many beautiful people a man could fuck before he got bored?

Five years ago, I would have said *never*. But now, after seeing the fierce, magnetic love between Ivy and Jules—someone who I never thought would fall in love again—I didn't know anymore. Because whatever they had was palpably vibrant and intoxicating, and no amount of strings-free fucking would come close to that.

Molly had seemed to sense it too, or maybe I was projecting, but after the first time we'd met Ivy and seen the tense string of connection between her and Julian, Molly started to withdraw.

Into her business, into herself, and I only saw her a handful of times last summer, usually in passing and always in groups of people. *Broken-hearted,* people said. *She'd always secretly loved Julian. It's no surprise she wants to avoid our crowd.*

But I wasn't sure. In fact, if I didn't know better, I would have said that she had been pulling away from *me*.

And then came that fateful day.

My hand went to my eye, as if about to probe a bruise, but the bruise had been gone for eight months now. Molly hadn't said that she never wanted to see me again, she hadn't said that she would never forgive me, but I had assumed all that was implied when she struck me.

And I hadn't said *I'm sorry.* I hadn't dropped to my knees and begged for her to forgive me, because I had assumed all that was implied when I'd let her strike me, when I'd turned away and left England.

I changed trains at the outer edges of London, settling in for the short ride to the station near Piccadilly Circus. And that's when I heard a familiar pair of tinkling laughs.

I turned to see Rhoda and Zona walking towards me down the aisle, the swaying motion of the train barely perturbing the movement of the graceful creatures as they made their way to my row and sat down in a flounce of expensive silk and lace.

"Ladies," I greeted them, taking their hands to kiss. "What marvelous luck to run into you on my first day back."

"Silas!" Rhoda exclaimed with a smile. Both she and her sister were studies in pale—pale skin, pale blond hair, pale gray eyes. They looked like twin Nordic goddesses, tall and beautiful, and I felt a familiar tugging in my groin as I remembered the last time we'd been together. Mercy had been there that night too…

Mercy Atworth was part of the reason I'd left the country, part of the reason behind my black eye all those months ago. She was also one of the most beautiful women I'd ever met.

Somehow, as if reading my mind and its tangled, depraved thoughts, Rhoda announced, "Oh, here come Mercy and Hugh."

I turned, my heart closing with something like panic while my dick started to stiffen, as if the two organs were controlled by different brains. What were the fucking odds? On this train, on this day, at this particular hour, that I should run into the one singular reason why Molly and I fought, why Molly and I never became a *we* or an *us*.

Which is a good thing, I reminded myself. *You don't love Molly. Maybe you never really did love her. It was a moment of weakness, a moment where you confused friendship with something more, and you should thank Mercy for proving that to both of you.*

Mercy Atworth smiled at me as she came closer, her black hair piled in rich coils on top of her head, her long eyelashes fluttering against ivory cheeks as she looked down and then up at me. Mercy was beautiful in a very physical sort of way; every feature and every curve could have been lifted entirely from a classical marble statue. But there was something about the secretive press of her mouth and the hooded veil of her eyelids that really made a man or a woman take notice. It was like she held ancient, esoteric knowledge, and she wanted you to come discover it inside her. She was seductive and silky and eager to please, and all of a sudden, I felt like Silas from last year, carefree and intent on fucking someone immediately.

Our gazes locked, and for one ridiculous moment, I imagined that I was staring into a pair of blue eyes instead of brown ones. That a different woman was walking toward me with that sultry smile on her face. And then I wanted to scream at myself. I came back because of Molly but not *for* Molly.

I came back with a business offer.

I wasn't in love with her.

At all.

Hugh Calvert handed Mercy into the seat next to me while he continued to stand. Like the sisters, Hugh was tall, fair, and blond, but in a rich, buttery sort of way. I'd never liked Hugh very much. He was a viscount—the only titled one among our set other than Castor Gravendon, whom we usually called 'The

Baron'—and even though we all had money to spare, there was something in his demeanor that indicated he felt slightly above us all. But Molly had liked him, and what Molly said went, at least for Julian and me, and so he'd become permanently fixed in our circle—for better or for worse.

"Silas," Hugh said coolly. "Back from France, I see."

Mercy was adjusting her skirts, and I felt the warm press of her leg through the fabric. "I had some things to take care of for Thomas," I replied, stretching my legs and giving Mercy my sunniest grin.

She smiled back.

"That's the only reason?" Hugh asked. I wasn't watching him, but I could practically hear his eyebrows rising.

I thought of the letter in my pocket. Surely they knew. Molly was a friend to all of us—well, maybe not to Mercy any more—but if Julian had heard about it all the way in Yorkshire, then everybody else here in London must know.

"Actually—" I started, but the train lurched to a halt.

"This is our stop," Rhoda and Zona said in unison, and Hugh nodded. "Mine too. I was going to escort Mercy to her house, but it's so close to yours, Silas…"

Delightful. I'd forgotten that Mercy's London house was a mere block from my own. This could prove very felicitous for me settling back into London life—and more importantly, for proving to myself once again that I wasn't in love with Molly, that I certainly wasn't pining for her.

"Of course, it would be no problem," I grinned. "As long as Miss Atworth doesn't mind."

"Oh, I am Miss Atworth now, am I?" Mercy teased from beside me.

In response, I took her hand and raised it to my lips. "Darling, I'll call you whatever you like."

"Marvelous," Hugh said, looking almost gleeful for some reason. I didn't like the look on his golden face; it seemed both smarmy and ominous somehow. "In that case..." He stood, offering his arms to the twins. "Shall we?"

"Bye, Silas!" the sisters chimed, and soon the whole party was gone from the car, leaving only Mercy and me. I met her gaze, feeling a jolt of lust mingle with a flash of pain. The last time we'd locked eyes, it had been moments before Molly had hit me. Our gazes had met as I'd felt Mercy coming around my cock, felt her body shivering with release. Then we'd heard the door open and Molly's footsteps across the floor as she walked into the room.

Locking eyes now was like locking eyes with the embodiment of my own shame and weakness. But it was also like I was Silas Cecil-Coke, notorious playboy, meeting the eyes of a beautiful woman. With a monumental effort, I pushed everything back down and focused on Mercy, who'd acquired a concerned expression under my stare.

"Are you upset with me?" she asked in a low voice. "Because of what happened with Molly?"

Fuck. The one thing I didn't want to talk about. I ran a hand through my hair. "Of course not," I lied. Charming Silas, polite Silas.

"Okay," she purred. "Good. Because I missed you. Did you miss me?"

Did I miss her? I looked at Mercy, pouting her red-lipped pout, and my erection strained against my pants. Fucking her had always been a pleasure, and it would be a pleasure right now, especially since it had been a few weeks since I'd partaken of the female sex, and the train car was empty save for us...

But *no*. No, I hadn't missed Mercy. Missing only belonged to one person. The one person I came back for.

Stop it, Silas. Shake it off.

"Yes," I lied again.

"Good," she said, and then she reached over and my lies faded from my lips. The moment her fingers brushed against my cock, it thickened, hungry for her, hungry for anyone, and then, alas, the train reached its stop.

"Here we are," she said.

I stood and helped her into the aisle. "Would you like me to escort you home?" I asked in her ear.

"I'd like you to escort me to bed."

Well, then.

The walk was short and hot, and I did my chivalrous best to keep Mercy under her parasol as we went. And then we were inside, and then we were in her bedroom, and then she unbuttoned her dress in short, efficient movements.

"Lie down," she ordered.

I complied, unbuttoning my trousers to free my erection as I did. I lay on my back, cock exposed, hands laced behind my head, and watched as Mercy swayed over to me. She was truly beautiful, especially naked, so very ripe and womanly and soft. But as she slid over me, as she positioned me and slid her pussy down my length, I was not struck by the pleasure or by her beauty or by the licentious delight of it all.

I was struck by boredom.

I don't mean that I was bored with sex necessarily—as Mercy rode me with her slippery undulations, my body responded precisely as it should. But I realized for the first time how transactional it all was, how very much like scratching an itch or eating breakfast. There was no real spirit here, no real playfulness, no passion.

And then out of nowhere, came the memory of Molly's face when she'd caught Mercy and me together.

God. Her eyes when she'd seen us. She'd been gutted.

And to think that just the day before I'd betrayed her, we'd spent the entire day fucking. Sweaty, dirty fucking. Her rose-pink nipples in my mouth. Her wet, wet cunt like a vise around my dick.

Above me, Mercy was still moving and struggling to get where she needed to be. Out of politeness, I helped, finding her clit with my thumb and coaxing an orgasm out of her. Her gaze never left my face as she came, but me, despicable scoundrel that I am, I kept my eyes shut when it was my turn.

And as I pulsed inside of her, it was Molly O'Flaherty I pictured riding me, Molly O'Flaherty with her perfect breasts and her perfect mouth and her perfect, powerful right hook.

CHAPTER 2

SILAS

The summer sun framed the Baron's mansion in hues of sugar pink and deep orange, and music and laughter spilled out of every open window and door. The air already smelled like Molly, like something sweet and spiced all at once, like cloves and champagne. It smelled the way she tasted whenever I kissed her.

Or maybe I was losing my mind. After my interlude with Mercy yesterday, I couldn't stop thinking about Molly in precisely the ways I had forbidden myself all those months ago. The silkiness of her inner thighs. The light, girlish trill of her laugh. The exacting—almost ferocious—way she went over the daily ledgers, pen in hand, striking out figures and numbers like a vengeful goddess of commerce.

I shook my head, scattering thoughts of her away from my mind like leaves before the wind. I'd visited the Baron for luncheon today, and he had mentioned the party and that he thought Molly might attend. I made my plan: I would go, make my business proposition and leave. No emotions, no touching. I would talk to her like I would talk to any other business acquaintance, and that would be the end of it.

Or so I thought. Because once I saw her, whirling in a cyclone of red curls and blue silk, cradled in Hugh's arms— goddamned *Hugh*—all of my careful, emotionless plans vanished.

～

MOLLY

There were three things I promised myself this morning when I woke up.

One, that I would find a way to defeat the board's ridiculous demands.

Two, that I would fuck someone tonight at the Baron's party, and fuck them hard enough to forget the awful mess my carefully ordered life had become.

And three, *number three*, that today was the day I would finally fall out of love with Silas Cecil-Coke. Silas, the callous, unforgivable prick who'd cozened me into caring about him.

Fucking jackass.

But today, like every other day since Silas had fled the country, number three wasn't going to happen. And number one wasn't going to happen.

So I'd be damned if I was going to give up on number two. The night was still young.

The Baron—properly known as Castor, Lord Gravendon— had thrown a large party tonight for no particular reason that I could discern, other than that he enjoyed throwing them and that he was bored. And even though I had more or less avoided the Baron's house since the fateful evening I'd discovered Silas buried to the hilt in Mercy Atworth, tonight I'd decided to make an appearance. After months of tense negotiating with the board, and weeks of would-be suitors flooding my parlor, all I wanted was a night of music and dancing and orgasms.

Was that so much for a girl to ask?

"You are pensive tonight," Hugh remarked, placing a flute of champagne in my gloved hand. "Is anything the matter?"

Other than the fact that I must either lose my company or be sold into a loveless marriage?

It wasn't my habit to lie, but Hugh had been one of my closest companions recently, and it was his polite attentions and willingness to listen to me rail against the board that had gotten me through these last few months. So I didn't want to ruin his night with my bitterness.

"Only the usual," I said, a bit dismissively, and took a short drink to hide my face.

A gloved finger came up and stroked my upper arm—bare in the sleeveless silk dress I wore. "We could go upstairs. I could help you relax."

I turned to look at him—handsome, blond, and healthy in the sort of way that rich men look healthy, which is to say suntanned and muscular from travel and hunting. He'd come to London a few weeks before the board had laid down their edict and had been with me the entire time since. He was good-looking and loyal, and I came every time we had sex—what better traits could a man possess?

So why didn't I want him tonight?

"Maybe later," I evaded. "I'd like to dance some more."

He hid his disappointment well. "Of course."

I didn't actually want to dance. I wanted to hold a man down and use his cock to drive away all the fears and worries of the day. I just didn't know if I wanted Hugh to be that man, for whatever reason.

But once the band began playing a lively waltz, I felt like I needed to shore up my excuse. I set my glass down and put my hand on Hugh's arm. "Shall we?"

He bowed and we drifted onto the floor, where he placed his

hands awkwardly on my waist and shoulders. Though he was sure on a horse, he was not a very practiced dancer, and I could tell the activity bored him.

"Molly," he said as we began turning in unison with the other dancers. "Have you given any thought to our conversation yesterday?"

Ah.

Yes.

I remember now.

This is the reason I don't want to take him to bed tonight.

"I have," I said carefully, keeping my eyes on the other dancers. The Baron was across the room, surveying the crowd, and I wished more than anything that I was next to him and not here talking with Hugh about the one thing I hated talking about.

"And?" Hugh prompted.

"And," I sighed, "I'm still thinking about it."

"What is there to think about?" His voice was friendly, but the words chafed me nonetheless.

"There's a lot to think about," I snapped. "This is my company, Hugh, and the rest of my *life*. Just because the board is forcing me to marry doesn't mean that I will wed just anyone."

We spun and stopped in time with the music, now side by side, and Hugh's mouth was at my ear. "But I am hardly just anyone, am I?"

That, I had to concede. After all, if I *had* to marry, wouldn't it be better to marry a friend? Someone I knew and didn't mind sharing my body with? Hugh had money and connections, and adding those to the company would be a fantastic business maneuver. It was certainly better than marrying one of the mustachioed sops that kept calling on me at all hours of the day.

So why was I holding back?

"Is it Julian?" Hugh asked.

I glanced to him, confused for a moment. "Julian...Julian Markham?"

"What other Julian is there?" he asked impatiently.

"What does he have to do with anything?"

Hugh's face pulled close to mine, so close that I could see the light from the chandeliers catching on his golden eyelashes. "Is he the reason you don't want to marry me? Are you still in love with him?"

A year ago—what felt like a lifetime ago—I might have said yes. I might have thought about those long Amsterdam nights, those shady Vienna days—weeks and months going from Paris to Rome to Brussels and everywhere in between, Julian and me and our friends. I might have thought of Julian's brooding features or the short growls he made as he came.

But the word *love*, the poetic, almost Biblical weight of it, revealed those faraway feelings for what they were—a schoolgirl's obsession, though I had admittedly carried it long past my schoolgirl years.

I knew the truth, even if I tried to forget it: what I had felt in three days with Silas was infinitely more than I had felt in ten years with Julian.

"No, Hugh," I said, meaning to sound dismissive, but instead sounding tired. "It's not Julian."

"Then who?" he demanded.

When had Hugh gotten so bloody pushy? He'd only just made his sort-of proposal yesterday, and he had been the one to encourage me to take my time deciding, since there were still a few months left to the board's deadline. Why did he feel the need to rush this all of a sudden?

I opened my mouth to deliver a sharp retort—a rebuke, really, because nobody talked to Molly O'Flaherty like that, least of all a potential husband—and then the dancers whirled, me along with them. The dance floor cleared into a pattern of even, straight rows, the kind of rows that meant you could look all the way across the ballroom and see the spectators standing at the edges.

See anybody standing at the edges.

Like, say, somebody tall, with dark hair and a dimpled smile. Somebody with wide shoulders and a narrow waist, both the shoulders and the waist hugged indecently well by a black tuxedo.

Blue eyes flicked to mine.

"Our babies would have blue eyes."

A lone finger ran up the plane of my stomach, past my breasts, past my throat. Rested near my cheekbone.

"You think I want babies?"

That irresistible grin. "With me, you do."

My satin heel caught against Hugh's foot and I stumbled. "Fuck," I swore under my breath, and then for good measure, "Fuck, fuck, fuck."

"What?" Hugh asked, helping me steady myself.

"Silas is here."

Hugh's shoulders grew stiff and his eyes narrowed. "Where?"

"At the far end of the ballroom." I could no longer see Silas, but my heart thumped as if he were right next to me, as if he were touching me...tasting me. Every nerve ending, every pulse point lit on fire at the mere idea of his proximity, and *oh God*, I could hear his laugh now, that fucking contagious laugh. I knew how he would look laughing too, his eyebrows lifted slightly as if he were taken surprise at his own happiness, his teeth white and flashing, his dimples so deep and lickable.

"I have to go," I said abruptly and pulled away from Hugh. Thankfully, he didn't fight me, and we exited the dance floor. I was shaking with adrenaline and rage and—Mother Mary help me, lust.

Overpowering, flaming, burning, scorching lust.

Stop. Think.

But I couldn't. I was too furious and too aroused, and the two sensations were so intertwined that I couldn't begin to peel them apart. Because how dare he fucking come here, to England, how dare he show his face in *this house* again, the very house where he'd broken my heart? And how dare he look so delicious and tempting in his tailored tuxedo, laughing as if he hadn't a care in the world? I wanted to scratch his back until it bled, I wanted to slap his face until my hand stung, I wanted him to pin my arms behind my back and bend me over and—

No.

Molly O'Flaherty didn't let men bend her over. She didn't let men fuck her—she fucked *them*, she rode them until she came and then she was done. And certainly she didn't let Silas do either of those things. Not any more.

My feet moved where my mind could not—away from Silas. I pushed angrily through the crowd, finally emerging onto the wide steps leading down to the Baron's garden, gulping the still-warm night air as if it were gin—which was something I desperately needed right now.

"Molly?" Hugh asked. "Would you like to leave?"

I braced my hands on the railing, looking out over the wide expanse of the Baron's estate, low green grass studded with bursts of flowers and capped by a large hedge maze at the end. "No," I said firmly. I didn't bother pretending I was upset about something else; there wasn't a fashionable soul in London who didn't know what had happened between Silas and me last year, and that included my would-be suitors. "I was here first. I am not leaving because of *him*."

"Well, you shouldn't talk to him," Hugh advised. "Let's just avoid him for the rest of the night. And I can find out from the Baron how long he plans on staying in London."

I hadn't even thought that far ahead—that he must be staying here in London, that all of my regular haunts might be extra haunted.

And now he was making me feel like I needed to hide in my own city—*damn him!*

My anger crystallized into something hard and cool. "Thank you, Hugh," I said calmly. "I so appreciate your thoughtfulness."

He gave me a small smile, the kind that could easily be called smug.

I laid a hand on his forearm. "Do you mind getting me another drink? The dancing overheated me."

"Of course." He leaned in and kissed my cheek, a gesture that felt oddly proprietary. I clenched my teeth together but made no reaction until he walked away, and then I gave the flagstones one hard stomp under my dress, like a little girl throwing a tantrum.

I didn't want to be kissed, I didn't want to be coddled, I didn't want to marry Hugh and I didn't want Silas to be here. I stomped my foot one last time, shook my shoulders to rid myself of the rest of my anger, and then stepped back into the ballroom, my face schooled into a placid mask.

I would find Silas. I would tell him to leave. And that would be the end of it. The end of my thrumming pulse and the end of the balled need in the pit of my stomach.

The night had grown late enough that some of the more unique elements of the Baron's parties were beginning to show. Skin uncovered, hair unbound. Dancing turning to kissing, kissing to fondling. I used to thrive in the midst of this, I used to be the princess of this scene, but now it merely irritated me. All these people basking in their frivolity, their escapism, and me stuck with my powerless, joyless future.

I pushed past them all until I reached the end of the ballroom, where I'd last seen Silas. I couldn't find him, and for a moment, I thought perhaps he'd left, and my heart soared at the same time as it split apart and withered.

"—Provence is always beautiful, although not as beautiful as you, darling."

I froze. And turned.

And right behind me, surrounded by a group of young tittering women that I didn't know, was Silas.

From this vantage, I could see the way his jacket stretched across his wide shoulders. The way it tapered into his lean hips, hips that had once dug into my thighs, hips that I had bitten and licked and tickled. I could see where the smooth skin of his neck met the dark brown of his hair. I could see the angle of his cheek

41

as he turned to survey the dance floor. His cheek was dusted ever so faintly with stubble, which was unusual for him, and unfortunate for me, because it only highlighted those high cheekbones and the square-carved symmetry of his jaw.

I swallowed. It didn't matter how square his jaw was or how delicious that neck would taste against my tongue. He was not welcome here.

I strode forward and touched his shoulder, opening my mouth to speak the words, but then he spun and his eyes were so goddamn blue. His eyebrows lifted as if he were about to grin that beautiful, terrible grin, and instead of speaking, I raised my hand and hit him across the face as hard as I could.

CHAPTER 3

SILAS

J suppose I shouldn't have been surprised that Molly slapped me. I deserved it, for one, and for another, the look we'd exchanged on the ballroom floor earlier had not boded well for our reunion. Not because she'd looked angry when our eyes met, but because she'd looked hurt.

What was surprising about the slap, however, was *my* reaction. I'd never been a man who'd liked things rough. I liked things pleasant and fun and easy. But in those three days I'd spent with Molly last year, something had happened. I had been fiercer and rougher with her than I had been with anyone ever before. And she—she had let me do things I would have never thought Molly O'Flaherty capable of letting be done to her.

And so when her palm sent fire stinging across my cheek, my dick thickened and my stomach tightened and something like a growl came out of my chest. And before I knew it, I was hauling her away from the crowd, my fingers wrapped around her wrist, the soles of her dancing shoes hissing against the polished wood as I pulled and she fought.

"Let *go*," she snarled, and since we had reached my destination—a small curtained nook near the foyer—I obeyed.

She crammed herself into the corner, silk bunching around her legs, and I yanked the curtains shut.

"How dare you—" she started, and then I strode forward and sealed my mouth over hers, swallowing her words along with the sigh that followed, a sigh that was anger and pain and surrender all in one.

Her mouth tasted like champagne and cinnamon, her lips were soft—softer than I remembered—but warm. When I parted them, her tongue was a slide of silk and heat, a sensation that went straight to my cock. It throbbed for that tongue, for that hot mouth. It wanted to violate her...again and again and again.

Molly's face tilted up to mine, exposing her throat, and I don't know how my hand found it, just that it did. And my hand caressed the smooth white column of her neck before I cupped her nape to keep her face tight to my own.

She pulled back, gasping, her breaths forcing her tits against her corset. I was so fucking hard right then, I swore I could feel every beat of my pulse in my dick.

"Don't touch me," she managed, trying to catch her breath. Her pupils were wide black pools and her lips were swollen. I dropped my hand from her neck.

I had no idea why I had dragged her off like a caveman or why I'd felt the need to brand her with such a possessive kiss. It had come from some dark place inside of me that I was unfamiliar with, despite the fact I'd seen it last year when I'd been with Molly. It had laid dormant since, but now that I was with her again, now that I had those pert, small breasts in front of me and all that scarlet, silken hair, and that adorable smattering of freckles across her nose—it flared back to life, roaring.

Take her, it urged. *Use her.*

Love her.

I shook it off. Donned the charming Silas mask everyone knew and loved. "Darling, I am so sorry. I simply couldn't help myself; you are such a rare vision tonight." I grinned at her, reaching out to run my thumb along her lower lip, but she swatted me away.

"Don't call me darling," she spat. "And don't pull that playboy shit on me. We both know better."

The dark thing reared its head again. "We do know better, don't we? How many times did you let me come in your ass, Mary Margaret O'Flaherty? And how many times on your face? How many times did you let me spank you until you were begging for more? Begging for me to ram my—"

"Stop," she said, her voice shaking. Her jaw was set, but her eyes glittered, unshed tears turning the bright blue eyes into dark sapphires. "Just stop."

I looked at her—really looked at her. At the delicate swoop of her nose and the fine china of her skin under her freckles. At the dark smudges under her eyes, as if she hadn't slept well in months, and at the angular dip of her collarbone. At the frail curve of her shoulders.

"You've lost weight," I said quietly, and the dark thing in me was pacing and angry. Not at her, but at *myself*. I felt the unaccountable urge to find some food and make her eat it in front of me. *She's your responsibility*, the dark thing said. *She is the woman you love, the woman you should be serving. The woman you should be doing everything in your power to care for.*

I pushed the voice down, down and away from my mind. "Molly," I tried again. "I'm so sorry. May we start over?"

She cleared her throat, not meeting my eyes. "I think you should leave."

"Leave the Baron's?"

She took a breath and then lifted her gaze, firm and still wet with tears. "No. Leave London."

Something jagged sliced through my chest. Jagged and cold.

"We ended badly," she continued, "but I see now that it was for the best. You and me—what we had—it wasn't real. It was only three days, and Silas, we know better than to believe in love. Whatever we said to each other, whatever we promised each other, it was delirium brought on by good sex and nothing more. And you did us both a favor by dispelling that delirium as quickly as possible."

The cold, jagged slice went deeper. "Dispelling it by fucking Mercy, you mean," I said hollowly.

She hesitated, her throat bobbing ever so slightly, a tiny tremor in her chin. "Yes," she said after a minute. "By fucking Mercy."

We stared at each other again.

"Molly—"

She held up a hand. "Don't. Just—whatever you were here to prove, you've proven it, okay? And I wish that I could rage at you, I wish that I could rain hellfire on your head, but I can't. Not tonight. You've won, Silas. Now take pity on me and leave. I have too much going on in my life to expend the effort it would take to hate you."

I felt completely sliced in two now, bleeding and severed. I had done this, I had earned this apathetic defeated tone, with my own weakness and cowardice last year. But tonight wasn't supposed to be about last year. It was supposed to be about a fresh start, a straightforward agreement.

Just say what you came here to say, you idiot. "Molly," I said, as contritely and also as charmingly as I could. "I came here to help you. Not to fight you."

She lifted an eyebrow. She didn't believe me, which was fair, I supposed, given our history.

I went on. "Julian told me about the board and their decision to make you marry."

She sighed, making a *yes...and?* gesture with her hand.

"And I came back from France because I want to help you."

"Silas," she said, "you can't help. No one can. I've seen every solicitor in London and there's nothing to be done. Their decision is in no way illegal. They have every right to sell their shares if they so choose, and even though using that to force me into marriage feels like blackmail, legally, it is not."

"I wasn't talking about solicitors, Mary Margaret," I said softly. "I was talking about me. Me and you. I came here to marry you."

Her mouth fell open into a small *O*, and the glimpse of her pearl-white teeth and pink tongue reminded me how stiff my erection still was, how much my skin still burned to touch hers.

"You want to *marry* me?" she asked disbelievingly. "Why?"

Because I love you.

Because I can't stop thinking about you.

Because I've found heaven, and it's you and your perfect mouth and your perfect pussy.

"Because I have a proposition for you," I said, still friendly, still smiling, still all business. "I can marry you, so you can satisfy the board's demands, and then I will never, ever interfere in your running of the company or allow the board to use me to coerce you in any way—even if we have to playact at me taking charge, I never will interfere. And then you give me what I want. A transaction. No emotions, no entanglements, simply an exchange."

"Exchange? Exchange for what?" Her tone was still doubtful, still incredulous. I knew that what I was about to say next would not repair that in any way.

I gave her the most dimpled and handsome smile I could muster.

"For a child."

Her skin went even paler than normal, chalk-white against the sandy ecru of her freckles. "A baby," she said, her voice devoid of any affect or feeling. "A…child."

"A human baby," I teased. "Yes."

She blinked. Stared at me. Like she'd never heard of babies before.

"You want a baby," she said, her face slowly changing from

flatly pale to flushed and suspicious. "You want to marry me so that...what? So that we have children together?"

"Yes."

She spun on her heel, realized she was facing a wall and then spun back. "Have you gone mad?"

"It's been a while since I checked, buttercup."

She didn't even crack a smile at my response. She stepped forward, her cheeks flaming scarlet. "Are you joking, then? Is this some sort of elaborate prank?"

"My offer is as serious as sin, Molly. I'm not insane and I'm not joking."

She came closer, so close I could smell her again, spices and the clean, flowery smell of her hair. "Then how *dare you*," she seethed. "How dare you come here after what you did and presume to think that I could ever—*ever*—entertain the idea of being bound to you. How dare you think that I would debase myself enough to marry you? To carry your fucking *child?*"

Her volume had risen with her color, and I was certain people on the other side of the curtain could hear her. She was magnificent right now, her hands balled into fists in her skirt, her hair tumbling around her shoulders, her slender frame visibly shaking with anger.

I hadn't expected her to hit me and I hadn't expected my very physical (and deeply wrong) response to her striking me—but this? This bone-rattling, blood-boiling rage?

This I had expected.

"I know we have a history—" I started.

"A *history?*" she shrieked. "A *history?* Is that what you call it? You told me you cared about me, Silas, you told me that you wanted me and me alone and that you were done being with other women. You saw me *crying!* I told you..." She faltered and trailed off, her gaze breaking away from mine, her thin arms wrapping themselves around her body. "I told you I loved you."

She didn't have to say any more. We both knew what had happened next.

"I won't try to defend myself," I said quietly. "I don't have any reasons or excuses except that I'm a loathsome troll." *And that I was scared to death of the way you made me feel.*

Of the way you still make me feel.

"But I don't think we should let this bad blood keep us from a mutually beneficial arrangement. You need a husband to appease the board, and I can be that husband, just for appearances' sake. We won't have to live as man and wife, and I won't ever involve myself in your business. It will be like we aren't even married, and then the board will have lost that particular bit of leverage over you."

"We won't have to live as man and wife...except you want a baby," Molly pointed out. Irritation and hurt still laced her words. "So you'll get to marry me and fuck me...and I am supposed to be grateful for it? For your charity?"

God, when she put it that way, it did sound terrible. "This isn't charity, darling, this is a mutually beneficial business arrangement. You need a husband. I want a family."

"And why do you want a family so badly, anyway?" she demanded, arms still crossed and eyebrow raised.

I didn't have a ready answer to that, not because I couldn't name all the reasons why I wanted one, but because it just seemed so...apparent. So obvious.

Who didn't want a family?

Molly. That's who.

I gestured to the curtain, where a chink in the fabric revealed a whirling tableau of dancing, drinking and sex. "Is this really all you want your life to be? Meaningless fucking and too much wine? You don't ever think about your future—about settling down and being content? You don't ever want to experience the kind of pure, unconditional love that comes with a family?"

She didn't respond. But she was listening. I could see it in the alert way she followed my movements, the way her lips pressed together at my words.

I decided it was time to be even more honest. I had been

thinking about this arrangement for a solid week now, and I had grown used to its unusual proportions and conditions. But I also appreciated that this was a lot for her to take in at once.

I stepped closer to her, expecting her to step back. But she didn't; she stayed where she was, even when I got so close that I could feel my shoes brushing against her skirt.

"I look at Thomas and at Charlotte, I see the life they have, and I want that, Molly. I don't want to be the playboy any more. I don't want to fuck forgettable women and drink too much and let my years pass me by. I'm thirty-five, and I'm too old to ignore how empty I feel. I want *more*."

The pulse jumped in her throat as her eyes flicked to mine. There was something there, something in those blue depths that reached out to me. A sympathy or an empathy or *something*—she knew how I felt. And maybe she felt the same way.

"And I know now," I continued quietly, "that I don't deserve to have the love of a woman. Not like Julian and Thomas have with their women. But maybe, just maybe, I can be a good father. Maybe I can have the rest, even if I can't have the marital bliss."

Her eyes closed for a moment, her dark red lashes resting against her cheeks, and God, I wanted to touch her again. I wanted her to tell me that I was wrong, that I did deserve to have the love of a woman and that I could somehow work to deserve hers again.

I wanted it more than anything.

But instead, she opened her eyes and shook her head. "No, Silas. I will not be your womb for hire."

Disappointment crashed heavy and cold into my stomach. I bit my lip and her gaze followed the motion. I was still hard, and the only thing I wanted more than her saying *yes* to my unconventional proposal was her saying *yes* to me lifting her skirts and devouring her pussy until she couldn't stand anymore.

I didn't pressure women into anything—proposals, sex, dancing, card games, *anything*—mostly because I'd never had to, but also because that wasn't me. I liked being easygoing. I liked avoiding conflict. I had told myself on the way here that if she said *no*, I would simply have to bear it up and leave. That I would honor her wishes.

But now that I was here, staring at the long arch of her throat and the blood-colored hair running over one shoulder, at those blue eyes so sad and strong and tired, I couldn't give up on her. I couldn't let her go that easily. Even if I didn't love her anymore, I had to face the fact that I *wanted* her. I had to face all the crass, caveman-like images wanting her conjured. I wanted her to be my mate, and the idea of another man claiming her instead made me see crimson splotches of rage.

I had to face it: no matter how wrong it was, I couldn't give up on marrying her. Not yet.

"Am I allowed to try to change your mind?" I said, leaning in so that my lips were near her ear.

She shivered, goose bumps prickling along her shoulders and arms, and I smiled grimly to myself. She wanted me still. After everything.

"Answer me, darling. Am I allowed to persuade you to marry me?"

My lips were at the shell of her ear now, and I nipped at her earlobe, drawing my teeth along the soft skin there before replacing them with my tongue.

She let out a half sigh, half moan.

"Maybe," she breathed, as I let my mouth wander down her neck, licking and savoring and sucking, her skin sweet and clean with the slightest hint of salt. It tasted better than I remembered, which made me think about the other things I had tasted and wanted to taste again. "Maybe," she repeated and then gave a little gasp as I gently bit her throat.

Good.

"Give me a word, Molly."

"W-what?" she stammered, and I loved that my mouth on her

skin made her incoherent. Maybe I had a shot at winning her hand after all.

"You know how this game is played, pet. You've played it here at the Baron's often enough. You choose a word. A signal. And when you use it, I will stop, no questions asked."

"We're not having sex tonight," she said, but she didn't sound very sure of herself, and her addition of the word *tonight*... I noted that and continued kissing her neck, working my way over to the other side and kissing up to her jaw.

"It isn't for sex. It's for pursuit."

She pulled back a little, her eyes narrowing as she tried to parse my meaning.

My hand found her skirts and I began pulling on the silk, lifting it up to her waist. "If I court you, if I try to marry you, I am going to use every dirty, filthy trick I know. If I try to win your hand, I am not going to play fair." Skirts up, petticoats raised, I dropped my other hand to run up the outside of her thigh. And then the inside.

Her legs fell apart and she slumped against the wall, her eyes fluttering closed once more as my fingers crept closer and closer to where we both wanted them most.

"For example," I murmured, "I could do this—" I swept my fingers up and across the soft flesh of her mound, carefully avoiding her inner folds or her clit, savoring the almost pained sigh she gave me. "And I could promise to put my mouth down there. You'd like that, wouldn't you? You would give me anything right now so long as I gave you my mouth in return."

A little noise escaped her, and then—my own self-control faltering—I cupped her. Hard. And even without penetrating her, I could feel how wet she was—dripping and slick—and *fuck*, my cock hurt. I wanted to make this woman come, and then I wanted to stick my cock inside of that swollen, tender flesh and drive away all the doubt and pain and blame we'd built around each other. I would tear it all down until she came like a quivering shot around me, and then I would fist her hair and press my crown against her mouth and make her lap up my cum as I pulsed it onto her lips.

I pressed a finger inside of her. She cried out, squirming, trying to grind her pussy down onto my hand. "How long has it been since you've let someone really fuck you, Mary Margaret? I know you've played, I know you've used lovers to get off, but how long since you've let someone use you?"

I slid my finger in deeper and added a second one, rubbing her hard with the heel of my palm. She was panting.

"How long?" I asked, wondering for a minute at my stern voice, at my almost-cruel words, but then she answered and I stopped caring how cruel I seemed.

"No one since you," she whispered.

I crooked my finger, creating friction against her favorite spot, and her knees buckled. I caught her by the throat, wishing I could somehow freeze the flash of fear and lust in her eyes, freeze it like a painting and then hang it on my wall.

God, this woman.

This woman.

She was making me forget that I wasn't supposed to be in love with her. She was making me forget that charming, happy, playful Silas would never grab a woman by the throat, never finger her without her express wish, and yet here I was, doing it anyway.

"See, my love?" I said, my fingers still curled around that gorgeous throat, my other hand rubbing her into a squirming and wet state of ecstasy. "See how I won't play fair? See how I'll touch you and tease you? See how I'll fuck you into giving me what I want?"

Her eyes flashed—indignation, perhaps, or maybe protest—but at that moment I squeezed her neck and ground my palm harder against her, and then a shuddering, buckling, slippery orgasm consumed everything in her. Her eyes closed, her mouth opened, a gasp for air that she could still get around my harsh grip but not without the illusion of struggle. And her sweet, wet cunt—I could feel it fluttering around my finger and all I wanted on this earth was to feel that fluttering on my tongue, one last time.

And it was amid her final crest, her last stunned sigh, that the curtains swept abruptly open, revealing Hugh.

CHAPTER 4

MOLLY

*M*y eyes flew open at the noise of the curtain, and there was Hugh, looking furious and alarmed all at once. The last shreds of my orgasm peeled away from my core and wilted, like flower petals in the summer heat. My mind began to clear, registering shame and horror and *oh my God, that was the best thing I've ever felt. Ever.*

Silas's hand was still at my throat, the perfect amount of pressure to send adrenaline zinging through my system without actually threatening my ability to breathe. And his other hand was still gripping my sex. And part of me never wanted it to leave. Part of me wanted to spend the rest of my life being so possessively held by this man, because somehow his arrogant manner of touching me sent me soaring far higher than even the most passionate caresses from any other lover I'd ever had.

The other part of me was simply furious. With *myself*, for having wanted Silas so much that I let him make me come. And with Silas, for being himself and yet not-himself, this new Silas that I had only glimpsed for the first time last year, and only then for a few days. This dominating, intimidating, rough Silas, who was more predator than gentleman.

This predator who counted me among his prey.

And Molly O'Flaherty is no one's prey, I thought fiercely.

I straightened to tell him this, to tell him that it didn't matter how dirty he played the game, he'd still never win me, when he was yanked backwards and Hugh's fist connected with his jaw.

I realized how it must have looked to Hugh, me backed into a corner, my skirts at my waist and Silas's hand around my neck. I suppose my gasps of pleasure could have looked like pain and the contortions of my face like a struggle—but still. No matter how well-intentioned his chivalry, it was unnecessary.

"Hugh!" I came forward, my skirts still in disarray, my breathing rapid and shallow from the intense climax I'd just had. I grabbed Hugh's arm before he could swing again. "Stop!"

Hugh threw me a furious look. "Molly, he...he was *touching* you."

I cleared my throat and smoothed my skirts, making sure that when I spoke, my voice was cool and collected. "He was touching me with my permission, Hugh. Step away."

Silas, meanwhile, was standing back up and rubbing his jaw with a rueful expression, like he should have expected all along that something like this would happen. "I have to say, Hugh, when I contemplated the possibility of leaving here with a bruise on my face, I rather thought it would be from Molly. At least you don't hit as hard."

Hugh practically snarled, lunging at Silas again. Silas easily dodged Hugh's second swipe, an arrogant grin spreading across his face. Now that the two of them were standing, now that Hugh was trying to hit Silas and failing, I could see that Hugh had gotten lucky with his first punch. Silas was tall and quick, and without any malice or apparent anger, he parried a punch from Hugh as he stepped in behind him. And then—almost casually—he twisted his body so that Hugh went sprawling onto the floor, landing hard on his ass.

And even though I still hated Silas, and even though I liked Hugh, I giggled, clapping a hand over my mouth when Hugh glared up at me. "I'm sorry," I said, the giggles punctuating the words. "I just—you look—I'm sorry."

Silas was trying not to laugh himself, at least until he turned to me, his bright blue eyes suddenly serious. "Molly. I need the word."

"The word?"

"Your safe word." Everything about his stare was too blue, too impossibly blue, and somehow hard and soft at the same time, like this look contained all of the love and all of the angry, resentful lust he felt for me. I remembered his fingers on my throat, and my cunt clenched with renewed want.

"You realize I am the first woman ever to need a safe word for courtship, right?"

His lips twitched, that irrepressible grin hiding under the surface, begging to come through. "If I'm honest, darling, this is the first time a woman has ever needed a safe word with me at all. But," and that beautiful mouth turned into something sterner than a smile, "this is also the first time I've ever wanted a woman to marry me."

Marry.

I'd repeated that word in conversation—and in my own mind —enough times that it didn't even sound real any more, like it was a word dredged up from some foreign and ancient text. A word synonymous with torture and pain.

I hated the thought of marrying, and the thought of marrying the one man who'd managed to break my heart...

"Clare," my mouth said before my brain could catch up. Before my brain could definitively tell my body—and my traitorous heart—that I didn't want Silas to have this safe word, because having it was tacit consent to his pursuit.

"Of course," he said, because unlike most people, he knew that I'd grown up in County Clare just outside of Ennis, until my father moved us to Liverpool when I was twelve. And I hated that he knew that. I hated how sweet and musical the word sounded on his lips when he repeated it: "Clare."

And then he gave me a deep bow and left, vanishing into the whirl of the wine-soaked ballroom almost immediately.

I glanced down at Hugh, who was finally standing up, and then to my wrinkled skirts. My body still sang from Silas's touch and the memory of those intensely blue eyes.

No, I told myself. *He doesn't get to come back here and parade those eyes and that easy grin around. That ship sailed—literally—last year.*

It sailed when I'd told him I loved him and when he'd said it back to me, and then I'd found him with his prick inside Mercy Atworth.

The memory sent a predictable storm of rage pounding through my blood, and I wished Silas were still here so I could rescind my safe word and finish the job that Hugh started when it came to layering that handsome face with bruises.

God, I needed gin.

Why I'd agreed to receive Frederick Cunningham the next morning, I wasn't entirely sure. Maybe I hoped the board had relented and he wanted to deliver the news in person. Or maybe I was sick of admitting anemic, floppy-haired dandies into my parlor and watching them plead their case for marrying me. Or maybe I was simply restless after seeing Silas last night, restless and furious and filled with an empty kind of longing. I'd gone home with Hugh, but I'd dismissed him the moment we crossed my threshold. He wasn't Silas, and no matter how much I wanted to pretend that my cunt didn't care, the lingering satisfaction in my body told me otherwise.

Whatever the reason I agreed, I immediately regretted it as I entered my parlor and Mr. Cunningham rose to take my hand.

The de facto leader of my company's board was taller and older than me, and I felt like a stupid girl in front of him.

A stupid girl of sixteen, to be precise.

The late morning light dusted his pale blond hair and matching mustache with gold, and the effect might have been handsome—for he was indeed a handsome man—if not for the smirk curling on his lips. I allowed him to kiss my hand, purely to show him that he had no power over me, but the moment his mustache tickled my skin, bile rose in my throat. The memory of stinging flesh and the taste of my own tears caused me to yank my hand away faster than was polite; Mr. Cunningham's smirk deepened as he rose back up to his full height.

Fucking hell, Molly. Show no weakness, remember? Be a wolf or a hawk or a snake—anything but the girl you used to be.

"How may I help you today, Mr. Cunningham? I'm afraid I have no husband yet, so if you're expecting my engagement announcement, you will be sorely disappointed."

"Call me Frederick, please. I think you've earned that familiarity, have you not, pretty girl?" Mr. Cunningham asked, settling into an upholstered armchair. *My* favorite armchair, if truth be told, because it sat at the head of the room. It was impressive and the perfect shade of blue to set off my eyes.

"I'd like to keep our acquaintance within the bounds of etiquette, if you don't mind," I said, doing my best not to grind my teeth together. I sat in another chair, one far enough away that I could pretend I didn't know what that mustache felt like on my skin. Far enough that I could pretend I didn't know exactly how selfish and ruthless he could be.

If I try to win your hand, I am not going to play fair.

Silas's words from last night echoed in my memory, and I forced myself to connect them to the man sitting across from me. Frederick Cunningham was exactly why I didn't let men fuck me, why I never ceded control of myself in the bedroom or in affairs of the heart.

Funny though, how I had so enjoyed the ruthless, selfish side Silas had revealed to me last night…

"As you may know, Martjin van der Sant is visiting us soon, and he will expect to meet with you, in addition to touring our docks and warehouses."

Van der Sant, yes. I'd almost forgotten in the fog of recent events, but van der Sant owned one of the most expansive shipping networks in the world, connecting Europe to India and China, and he was looking to partner with O'Flaherty Shipping in order to expand his reach to Iceland and Canada—places where O'Flaherty Shipping was established and thriving. A partnership between us would be mutually beneficial and profitable, with very few drawbacks. However, we needed van der Sant far more than he needed us, since we were already losing clients who wanted more access to the Eastern hemisphere, and he was a notoriously fastidious and uncompromising businessman. There had been at least two other English companies he'd come close to making an agreement with, only to pull out at the last minute because he didn't like the state of their books or the personal habits of one of their dock managers. Everything would need to be perfect for his visit, but I wasn't concerned. I ran O'Flaherty Shipping meticulously. There would be no irregularities in our books, our managers were all hardworking and moral men, and I was prepared to be as discreet as possible about my own personal habits when he came to town.

I took a deep breath and returned my attention to Mr. Cunningham. "I'm quite prepared for van der Sant's visit, a fact of which I'm sure you're aware. Is there another reason you needed to see me?"

He crossed his legs, raising his chin and looking quite pleased with himself. "I came to strike a bargain," Mr. Cunningham said.

"I am sick of your bargains," I said, not bothering to hide the irritation in my voice.

Mr. Cunningham smiled. "What a shame. But I think you will like this one better than our last."

Our last. To an outsider, it might have seemed that he was referring to the board's demand that I marry, but we both knew better. I kept myself from crossing my legs reflexively, making sure my back was straight and my shoulders square.

"In fact," he continued, "I am certain you will like it. Perhaps too much; I admit, it does feel as if the board will be ceding too much in this agreement."

Hope, for however brief a moment, flowered within me. As much as I hated this man, as much as I resented the other men who had invested in my father's company, perhaps something had happened to change his mind. Perhaps they had found a new heiress to torture or perhaps they'd realized I would still find a way to run the company the way I wished, even with a husband.

Not for the first time, I cursed myself for not having the money to purchase as many shares as possible. But a few years ago, I had sunk most of my money into long-term land investments in America and Australia, all of which were doing quite well, but by the time I withdrew my earnings and tried to buy out the shares, it would be too late and the deadline for my marriage would have passed. And even if I could, I knew the board members would not sell their shares to me, out of avarice or spite or some combination of both.

I should have been buying shares all along, I thought regretfully, and not for the first time. If I owned the majority of the shares, I wouldn't stand to lose so much when other people sold theirs.

"I'm afraid I still want you to get married," Mr. Cunningham said, interrupting my internal cycle of hope and regret. "Just to forestall whatever you might be thinking." Light glinted off his wedding band, and again, my sadistic memory dredged up the way it had looked in the candlelight of his room that night. The way it had looked covered in my blood and his semen when he'd shoved his fingers inside of me to confirm that yes, my hymen was well and truly gone.

My face burned with anger and my hands balled in my skirts, but I managed to keep my voice cold. Sneering, even. "I didn't dare to hope for anything of the sort, Mr. Cunningham. Please proceed; I have many other things I need to accomplish today."

"Very well then." He leaned back and uncrossed his legs. "I know how much you despise this parade of suitors marching through your door and crowding you at parties. I know you hate the idea of getting married and would like to have this matter settled as soon as possible. Which is why I have selected a suitor for you. He is willing, he is powerful, and he has the board's full approval. You will marry him and assume your proper role as a wife, and we will keep our shares, and everybody will live happily ever after."

"What," I asked, my voice icy, "makes you think I'd even be willing to consider someone of *your* choosing?"

"Frankly, Miss O'Flaherty, the board is being very magnanimous here: this gentleman is already a good friend of yours— and if I'm reading things correctly, he's sometimes been more than a good friend. He approached the board and has told us in good faith that he will assist us in our cares."

A good friend. My mind flashed to Silas and something in my chest squeezed. He'd said he'd playact with me in order to convince the board that I was doing his bidding; was this part of that? Had he already begun his pursuit of me? And why did that make me feel so light-headed and breathless?

"Who is it?" I demanded.

Mr. Cunningham dusted a speck of lint from his trousers. "Viscount Beaumont, Hugh Calvert."

"Hugh." Disappointment deflated me, helplessness streamed through my blood.

Hugh.

Hugh had approached the board, not Silas.

What did you expect? You know you can't count on Silas for anything. You can't trust him.

I forced myself to think clear-headedly. To be pragmatic. "Viscount Beaumont has already offered his hand to me."

"Splendid!" Mr. Cunningham said. "Well, perhaps I am late with this news then. When shall you be delivering your acceptance to him?"

Pragmatic Molly cautioned me to keep the hot, angry words from spilling out, words that would tell Frederick Cunningham exactly how long it would take me to deliver my acceptance to any man, which would be when hell froze over, thawed and then froze again.

No, Pragmatic Molly recognized that she'd already given Hugh's offer serious consideration. She recognized that perhaps this was the best chance she had at salvaging this miserable scenario and at least getting married to someone pleasant, someone who wasn't after her money.

"I'm still thinking about it," I said finally. "I am not willing to make this decision in haste."

"Very well," Mr. Cunningham said, shrugging and then standing to leave. "But just so you know, you may cease with interviewing your other would-be husbands. The board is quite set on the viscount."

"So I don't even have a choice now?"

Mr. Cunningham approached me, but I stayed sitting, my hands curled around the armrests, my fingernails digging in and denting the wood there.

"Oh, Miss O'Flaherty. *Molly*—you never minded when I called you Molly, did you? You always have a choice."

He stood right in front of me now, but I refused to stand or even to look up at him. Instead, I stared resolutely ahead at the large bay window overlooking Eaton Place, my jaw set.

Still, out of the periphery of my vision, I could see him unbuttoning his trousers, could see him withdrawing his penis.

Tears pricked the back of my eyelids, but I refused to let them spill. Not this time.

"You know what your choices are, don't you, Molly?" he asked, his facade of gentleness too weak to hide the triumph in his voice.

I didn't answer, didn't even shake my head, and then his hand was fisting my hair and his erection was at my lips, pressing, but I didn't open my mouth. He pulled my hair harder and tears did leak out now, but I still refused to accept what he was forcing on me.

"Be my whore," he said and I could hear him lick his lips. "Be mine, and I'll make everything else go away."

Somewhere in the back of my mind, I heard a sixteen-year-old girl crying and the sound of a pen nib scratching on paper. A decision that had saved my father's fledgling company and destroyed my innocence in one fell swoop.

"Come on," Mr. Cunningham coaxed. "I hear what a little slut you are. Am I supposed to believe that I have the one cock in London you won't suck?"

I knew better than to open my mouth to answer; he would only see that as an invitation, and I'd be gagging on his penis before I could get the first word out. While we'd never repeated the trauma of That Night, he had forced himself on me in other ways in the intervening years.

Part of me longed to bite his member as hard as I could, longed to see if I could bite it clean off. Another part wondered how much it would hurt if I grabbed his balls and squeezed until something ruptured. And yet another part of me—a small, defeated part—was tired of fighting him. Wanted merely to let him use me and leave so that I could move on with my life.

But whatever my fantasies were, I knew that Mr. Cunningham held all the power here. If I hurt him now, he'd have me arrested as fast as he could find a police officer. If I hurt him now, not only would he make sure that everything Father (and later, I) had built was taken away, but it would mean all my earlier sacrifices were invalidated. And that idea was just as repellent as doing his bidding, the idea that all of this debasement and humiliation had been for nothing.

He was breathing fast now, stroking himself as I still refused to open my mouth. "It's been a while since we've done this, Molly. How long has it been? A year?"

Eight months, two weeks and three days.

I only knew that because it was the day Silas had found me crying in this very parlor. I hadn't told him what had happened, I hadn't given him any sort of explanation, and after it became apparent that I couldn't be soothed in any of the normal ways, he'd carried me up to my room and my bed. He'd erased every tear with his lips, every foul taste with his own sweet tongue, used his hands and his cock to chase away the disgusting, used feeling I always had after Cunningham.

For whatever reason, thinking of that day, thinking of Silas and his tender blue eyes as he'd made love to me made me stronger. No, I wouldn't open my mouth today. Maybe I wouldn't fight back, but I wouldn't give in. I would find another way.

My refusal only seemed to arouse Cunningham further, as he moved his hand faster over his prick, and then with a soft noise, cum dribbled out of his tip and dripped onto my dress. I finally looked up at him, meeting his eyes for a moment before glancing meaningfully down at his fast-softening cock.

"If you're finished, I'd like you to leave," I said.

He gazed down at me, his eyes cold. "I think I got the answer I needed." He reached down and used my dress to scrub the remaining globules of cum off his flaccid cock, and it was only the vivid image of getting arrested for assault that stopped me from jumping up and ramming my fist into his teeth.

"Oh, I love seeing you so angry," he said as he let the ruined silk fall from his hand. "I am almost happy that you didn't choose to become mine—this way it will be so much more fun to see your husband break you."

"Hugh would never," I countered.

"Maybe not, maybe not," Mr. Cunningham conceded. "Regardless, I expect to hear your engagement announcement to the viscount very soon. The board is getting impatient." He gave me one last look. "I prefer my women fresher anyhow. Untainted. Younger."

I didn't bother seeing him out. Instead, I stood and tore at my dress after he left until my lady's maid scurried in to help—together we stripped it off and consigned it to the kitchen fire.

CHAPTER 5

SILAS

*S*eeing my solicitor and banker had taken all morning and all afternoon, and by the time I left, the day was already fading into a hot evening, accompanied by a listless breeze and the racket of carriage wheels on the road.

I had wanted to spend the day otherwise. I told myself that I'd wanted to spend it meeting up with friends and acquaintances, but truthfully, I'd wanted to spend it with my face under Molly's skirts. I'd left the Baron's last night with a raging erection that refused to abate, despite the two times I'd stroked myself off. Last year—hell, even last week—I would have found a woman to take care of it. I would have charmed her into my bed and fucked her until we were both limp and sweaty.

But for reasons I couldn't quite articulate to myself, I abstained. I settled for my hand and then woke up as hard as an adolescent boy as a result (and was forced to settle for my hand again.)

So I was already miserable this morning when I heard the

rumors at a breakfast with Rhoda and Zona, rumors that infuriated me and frustrated me and made me even more miserable.

Hugh and Molly. About to be engaged.

Thus the trip to the solicitor's. *Contingency plans*, my father used to tell Thomas and me as he managed the business of our estate. *The secret to success is to always have a contingency plan.*

And so here I was. Contingency plan in place, although I desperately hoped it wouldn't be necessary.

I didn't feel satisfied, or even relieved, as I took a cab back to my townhouse, mostly because things were still so uncertain. There were only *rumors*, hearsay, the one thing that travels faster than the wind. And since this Mr. Cunningham I'd wanted to meet with had decided that our meeting should be put off until tomorrow, I would have no real answers until then.

It wasn't until we pulled onto my street that I realized there might be someone else who had real answers, someone close to me.

Which was how I ended up in Mercy Atworth's house, waiting for her in her front room, pacing the rug with long strides. I practically jumped on her the moment she entered, but I backed away when I noticed she was wrapped in a silk dressing gown and nothing else.

My groin—already aching from last night's neglect—filled with blood.

"Silas, how unexpected. And wonderful. I'm sorry it took me a couple minutes, I needed to send word to a friend about something." She raised up and kissed my cheeks in the Continental fashion, her nearly-bare breasts brushing against my chest as she did, the thin silk of her wrapper doing nothing to hide the erect peaks of her nipples.

I took a step backward. And then deciding that wasn't enough, spun around on the pretense of examining the clock on her mantel.

"What brings you here today?" she asked. "Are you lonely

already? I figured there would be plenty of women at the Baron's who—"

"You're close with Hugh, aren't you?" I interrupted her. "I mean, you spend lots of time together. You were on the train together two days ago."

Mercy cocked her head a little, her hair sliding easily over her silk robe as if her hair were made of silk too. "Yes. We are close. Why?"

"Has Hugh offered to marry Molly?" I couldn't keep the urgency out of my voice, and I didn't really see the point in trying anyway. Soon, everybody would know what I was after here in London.

"*Oh*," Mercy said, her eyes widening as if suddenly everything had become clear to her. She walked over to a sofa, and I tried not to notice the enticing way her ass and hips moved under her dressing gown. She sat and patted the seat next to her.

I obediently sat down, trying to keep as much space between us as possible, even as my cock lengthened down my pant-leg, as if trying to reach for her.

"Yes," she said. "Hugh has proposed to Molly."

I swore.

"And..." she looked a little hesitant "...he also approached the board of her company and got their approval. He's the endorsed suitor for her hand now."

I let out a long breath between my teeth. *Fuck.*

Fuck fuck fuck.

Hugh—I should have fucking known from the possessive way he acted at the Baron's. I should have known he was doing more than escorting Molly for the night. He wanted to marry her.

"She hasn't said yes," Mercy said soothingly. "He proposed two nights ago, and she still hasn't given him an answer."

"She hasn't said yes?" I repeated, hardly daring to believe it to be true.

Mercy nodded.

"The board," I said. "Do they really support him? Can they force Molly to marry him?"

Mercy looked thoughtful. "I suppose it depends how badly Molly wants to keep her company afloat. Marrying is her only way to save it, and if Hugh is the only man they want her to marry..."

My face must have fallen, because she laid her slender hand on my shoulder. "But maybe she'll decide her independence isn't worth it and abandon her company. Or maybe she'll stay and let them sell all of their shares. There's no way it would stay solvent after the board left, but maybe she can start something new?"

I shook my head. "You don't know Molly. You don't know how much she loves that company—it was everything to her father, and now it's everything to her. She'll die before she gives it up." My heart clenched. Was this it, then? Was this the death knell to my courtship, ringing out its demise before it had ever even started?

"Maybe you can meet with the board," Mercy suggested. "And get them to change their minds?"

I did have a meeting with Frederick Cunningham tomorrow, the man I understood to be the informal leader of the board. "Maybe," I said doubtfully. "It has to be worth a try. I guess if it had to be anyone, Hugh isn't the worst. At least I won't have to worry about him taking advantage of her and her company since he has so much money already—"

Mercy snorted and I looked at her. Her face straightened immediately, and she leaned forward, letting her dressing gown fall open. Heavy, ripe tits spilled out, the nipples dark and hard.

I shifted, my dick surging at the same time as my mind remembered Molly's eyes last night, the gloriously furious way she'd yelled at me.

God. It was like I was two different people, and I wanted to be the good one, the one who only wanted one woman. *Why couldn't I just be the good one?*

"You must really care about Molly," Mercy said, her hand

moving from my shoulder to my chest, from my chest to my abdomen. Her dressing gown opened further, exposing the smooth, soft planes of ivory skin and the tiniest glimpse of dark, silky curls at the bottom. "I never thought I'd see the infamous Silas Cecil-Coke wanting to marry."

"It's a business arrangement," I said automatically. My mind was chanting *get away get away get away.* "A partnership between friends."

"You really know how to woo a girl," Mercy teased and then her hand was lower and lower and *fuck* that felt good.

"Oh, dear," she murmured. "You're so hard. Silas, you poor thing."

You know what? I *was* a poor thing. The woman I wanted didn't want me, and she was probably about to marry a man I despised, and I would never be able to find anyone like her again, and I was so hard that I couldn't think straight.

I gave Mercy a pouting look.

She moved like water, like satin folding against itself, smooth and silent, until she was kneeling on the floor in between my legs, looking up at me with dark eyes.

But when she reached for the buttons of my trousers, I stopped her, breathing hard. "Mercy, I want this, believe me I do, but it's not right for me to do it when—"

Mercy raised an eyebrow. "When what? When Molly went home with Hugh last night? When Molly has been fucking him the entire time you were away in France?"

Jealousy only made my dick harder. "*Shit,*" I hissed as she ran a palm over my length.

"And didn't you fuck women in France?" Mercy asked. "What's so different now?"

Because I've seen Molly again.

Because I've told her I want to marry her.

Because no matter how many women I fucked in France, I could never forget that Molly was the one I really wanted.

But the words had trouble making their way to my mouth.

Because she was stroking and squeezing me, and it felt so goddamn good, and maybe, if I was a little honest, I wanted revenge in some way. I wanted to erase the image of Molly and Hugh together with the image of me coming in Mercy's mouth.

She unbuttoned my trousers, and I raised my hips to work them down far enough to free my cock, and then there it was, veined and rigid, framed against Mercy's beautiful face and luscious lips, and then all of a sudden, they were on me, around me, and my cock was in a bed of wet, hot suction.

My balls drew up, my body ready to release the intense ache I'd been carrying since I impaled Molly's cunt on my fingers last night, but my heart was pounding in my chest—not the pleasant thud of impending climax, but the sickening thud of *wrong wrong wrong.*

I didn't want this silky brunette between my thighs. I wanted my redhead, freckles and temper and voracious sexual appetite and all. And I didn't want impersonal release. I wanted to soar *with* Molly, I wanted her blue eyes locked on mine as I came. I wanted to fall asleep wrapped around her slender body, and I wanted to wake up before she did so that I could pamper her with tea and breakfast.

I *did* love Molly.

And I didn't want anybody else.

Oh my God. *I didn't want anybody else.*

It was so obvious, so blatantly apparent, and yet I had missed it. I had blamed my unhappiness on a variety of reasons, blamed the lackluster sex on the women and my boredom, and all along repeated my mantra: *I don't love Molly O'Flaherty.* But who crosses the Channel and tries to marry someone they don't love?

"Mercy, stop," I said. And when she didn't, I placed my hands on either side of her head and lifted, my dick stone-hard and wet as her mouth left it.

"Mercy," I said again, ignoring the voice that told me to stick my cock right back in her mouth and fuck her throat until this erection was finally vanquished. "I really like you. But I just can't. I'm sorry."

But she wasn't listening to me. She wasn't even looking at me. She was looking past my shoulder at the entryway to the parlor, her expression surprised, and then I turned my head to see Molly standing there.

I stood abruptly, which was an idiot move, since my cock was still out. It was still hard, and worse, still wet from Mercy's mouth, and now on full display for Molly, who looked murderous.

Maybe murderous wasn't the right word. She looked like she could obliterate worlds, like a wrathful god, and every self-preservation instinct I had told me to run away. I had no interest in once again testing the boxing skills an impoverished Molly had learned as a girl in the gutters of Liverpool.

Instead, I buttoned myself up and walked towards her, debating what to do. After all, I'd told her when I'd proposed that we wouldn't have to live as man and wife, and clearly since she was cavorting around with other men, she didn't feel the need to prove her loyalty to any one person, so why should I? Our group had never been about sexual exclusivity. Even Julian had shared Ivy with our friends and me.

On the other hand, I had just realized something important, something huge, and it meant that I *had* betrayed her. I loved her and I let another woman put her mouth on me. Not just any woman, either. The woman who had driven us apart the first time.

Guilt crawled up my spine and lodged itself in my throat.

I stopped just short of striking distance, deciding on cautious honesty. "Molly, I can explain. But before anything else is said, you need to know that I—"

Hugh stepped out from behind her, and it was clear he'd been hovering out of sight the whole time. The pompous needledick.

"Silas," he said, sliding an arm around Molly's waist. "Fancy seeing you here. How's your face feeling?"

I wanted to rip his throat out. "Marvelous. Look, it didn't even bruise." I tilted my jaw so he could see how little damage his punch had actually done.

He looked sour, and that give me the smallest micron of pleasure. I turned my attention back to Molly, trying not to notice the way Hugh's fingers splayed against her rib cage, trying not to think about them going home together last night, trying not to think about her fucking him like I so wanted her to fuck me.

"Molly," I tried again. "This—I know this looks bad. And it is bad, I'm not denying that, but I realized something when Mercy was…" I trailed off. *Fuck.* There was no way to have this conversation without completely driving home the fact that I'd been, once again, caught fooling around with Mercy Atworth.

Molly didn't say anything to fill the silence, but she met my eyes, and what I saw there punched me in the chest. Pain and betrayal and rage, and the same deep, deep sadness I'd seen in her last year. The kind of hopeless despair that seemed so unlike her.

"Will you say something?" I pleaded. I was used to people talking to me, I was used to people smiling and laughing around me, and I had no idea how to handle this silence. This stone wall of O'Flaherty. *Say something, you idiot. Make her laugh or make her blush or make her mad—anything is better than this silence.*

I decided just to go for it. To just tell her. "Molly, I love you."

If the words sounded grand and important in my head, if I imagined them accompanied to music like they were part of a Gilbert and Sullivan show, I would never admit it to another soul, because in reality they came out weak and defensive and a tad bit manipulative. They in no way sounded noble or heartfelt or even genuine—they sounded like a kid telling his parents he loved them to avoid a strapping.

Molly responded predictably; whatever despair had been there before was now entirely wiped out by a fierce anger. She stepped forward, and it was only with great courage that I held my ground, bracing myself for the inevitable strike. But she didn't hit me. Instead, she leaned forward and said in a voice so low that I knew only I could hear it:

"Get. Out."

"Molly—"

"*Clare*," she seethed.

Clare.

Fuck.

With one last glance—a glance that was more like a glare on her end—I left.

CHAPTER 6

SILAS

I met Frederick Cunningham over lunch at the Cafe Royal. The venue was my choice, as it was primarily frequented by a younger, more fashionable set than Mr. Cunningham was likely used to, and I wanted him to feel out of place. I also wanted to meet him on familiar ground. Home territory.

I watched his face crease with distaste at the ornate pillars and brightly frescoed ceilings, and at the women dining beside men, all in a jostling swarm of Bohemians, journalists, and military officers.

Good.

The more unsettled he was, the more defensive he'd be. And defensive people often revealed their weaknesses.

I stood to shake Mr. Cunningham's hand as he approached, and then we both sat down, him appraising the restaurant while I casually appraised him. Mid-forties, good-looking— a little prettyish for a man. Undoubtedly wealthy, given the expensive cut of his suit and the fob watch gleaming under his jacket. But as I watched him condescendingly place his order and then sip tiny, Lilliputian sips from his wine glass, I deduced that whatever power he held came solely from his money and nowhere else. He didn't possess an innate respect for his fellow man—which meant that underneath his arrogance, there was a deep-seated and unconscious insecurity. And nothing about his carriage or demeanor belied anything but bored derision. No intelligence, no perception, no idea of his own soft spots. No inherent strength of will.

Plus, he drank his wine like a child, and I made it a point never to trust people who were weak drinkers.

"So, Mr. Cecil-Coke, to what do I owe the pleasure of this meeting? I was rather surprised to receive a letter from you, given that we haven't been previously introduced."

I'd kept my letter requesting our meeting purposefully vague, mentioning only that I had a lucrative business proposal for him. I'd done it because I wanted to see his face and hear his voice when I mentioned Molly. I wanted to know how he felt about her. Contemptuous? Jealous? Completely neutral?

I leaned forward, smiling as widely as I could. I wasn't unaware of the effect I had on men as well as women. Beyond the sexual, I'd always found that people responded much better to friendly charm than to brooding threats. (Which was the reason I'd always had more friends than Julian Markham.)

"Mr. Cunningham, I've heard that you and your company are looking for a man to marry Molly O'Flaherty. I would like to be that man, and I want to discuss terms with you to see how we can make that happen."

Mr. Cunningham blinked for a minute, and in that minute, I saw everything I expected to see—scorn and avarice and a glint of lust. "Well, Mr. Cecil-Coke, I'm sorry to say that you are too late. The board has already approved of a suitor."

"I heard. The Viscount Beaumont."

His blond eyebrows lifted. "You know that? Where did you hear that?"

"Mutual friends," I said vaguely. Until our lunch was finished and he inevitably hunted down any and all information about me, I didn't want him to know how close I was to Molly, since I suspected that would work against me at the moment. Let him just think I was a run-of-the-mill suitor chasing after an inheritance.

He made an indeterminate noise. "Mutual friends, you say."

"What did the viscount offer you?" I asked. "If it's money, I have plenty. If it's connections, I have plenty of those, too. Just name your price—and then any extra you would like to keep for yourself beyond that—and it's yours."

He narrowed his eyes. "Why are you so eager to wed Miss O'Flaherty? Maybe you don't spend much time in London, but her...ah, *spotted*...reputation is quite well known among certain circles here."

"My own reputation is quite spotted, Mr. Cunningham," I replied, not bothering to tell him that Molly and I had earned most of those spots together. "I'm not threatened by not having a virgin bride."

Mr. Cunningham actually shuddered. "I can't imagine. I made a physician ensure my wife was a virgin before we were married."

I was beginning to hate this man—and I hated very few people on this earth.

"And so I presume that you were also a virgin on your wedding night?" I said easily, giving him a smile as my eyes conveyed exactly the amount of dislike I had for him.

"Don't be ridiculous," he huffed. "It is a man's natural inclination to—"

I interrupted him. "Mr. Cunningham, about my offer— please. What will it take? Tell me your price."

I didn't have fathomless funds, but between myself, Thomas and Julian—and possibly even the Baron—there wasn't a number that I was afraid of this man naming. And yes, there was the small issue of Molly hating me more than ever after Mercy's house, but now that I knew I loved her, how could I stand idly by and watch her corralled into marriage with Hugh?

I had to act.

Mr. Cunningham wasted no time cutting into the steak the waiter set before him, and I could see him savoring both the meat and the words he was about to say.

"There is no price, Mr. Cecil-Coke, no amount of money that you could pay me or the board to change our minds. We are very, very set on the viscount marrying Miss O'Flaherty."

I nearly choked on the bite I'd just taken, hiding my surprise with a drink of wine. "Really?" I said evenly, after I'd swallowed and regained control of my thoughts. "No price at all? You must like this viscount very much."

A slyness slipped over his features. "We do, Mr. Cecil-Coke."

I didn't answer him, partly because I was still shocked he hadn't responded to my bribery. But also partly because a new suspicion was igniting, one I couldn't quite articulate, but one that spoke of a connection between Hugh and this man.

"And why is it that you like him so much?" I pressed. "I must know."

"He is simply the right fit for the company."

"And I suppose it doesn't matter who is the right fit for Miss O'Flaherty?"

Mr. Cunningham scoffed. "This has never been about individual needs, Mr. Cecil-Coke. This has been about the company, and what is necessary to keep it profitable in the long term. And the answer is not to have a woman dictating decisions simply because she owns a majority of the shares. She needs to be bridled."

I planned on being the only man to put a bit between her teeth, and even then, it would only happen in the bedroom and with her begging for it. "And what decisions is she making that are so detrimental to O'Flaherty Shipping Lines? If you don't mind me asking."

He dabbed at his mustache and upper lip with a napkin.

"She's soft-hearted, like a woman. She pays the dockworkers too much and the investors too little. She gives the workers Sundays and holidays off—she even gives them a break for lunch! When I think of the money that could be saved if we merely dropped our wages to what our competitors pay..." He shook his head. "It's appalling. But when she marries, the shares will legally belong to her husband. And then we will be able to move forward without all the..." he waved a hand around the table "...interference."

"I see." And I did see. This man was reprehensible. And the board was equally so, if they all thought like him. I felt a spike of pride for Molly, who had battled Mr. Cunningham and his friends in order to run the company the way she wanted. Who had run her company generously and ethically. All those years we'd spent lolling around Europe, petting and playing with each other, she'd also been contending with this board. She'd been single-handedly wrangling control of her company, and I'd never had any idea.

"And so you believe the Viscount Beaumont will be of service to you, then? More than I could be? Because I would certainly help you in your goals as much as possible."

I thought I sold the lie rather well, but Mr. Cunningham simply shook his head and sipped the last of his wine. "We've already found our man, and there's no changing our minds at this point. And with that being said, I'm not sure there is much more to discuss," he informed me as he stood. He tossed his napkin onto his half eaten steak. "Thank you for lunch."

I inclined my head but didn't stand. I wasn't sure I would be able to restrain the urge to bury my thumbs in his eye sockets if I did. "It was my pleasure," I said instead. "It was most enlightening."

~

MOLLY

It had been four days since I went to Mercy Atworth's house and found her sucking Silas. Four days and I was still furious.

And the worst thing? I wasn't even furious with Silas. I was furious with myself.

I walked through the Baron's hedge maze more or less aimlessly, cataloging all the ways I'd been stupid in my life. And most of them involved Silas.

Did you really think he had changed? Did you really think he meant all those things he said, those sincere-sounding things, and meant them so much that he would forget about any woman other than you?

But the problem was that I hadn't realized that I did think those things until it was too late. I had thought myself so blasé, so indifferent, and then I saw Silas with Mercy and discovered that all along I'd been harboring the hope that something had changed. That maybe he'd arrived here in London just in time to whisk me away from this nightmare.

Oh, how wrong I'd been.

And then he had the nerve to tell me that he loved me!

A little scream of frustration tore from my throat, and I kicked at the hedges with every ounce of strength I could muster, which only resulted in getting my skirt and my new white boot tangled in the tiny, twisting branches.

"Fuck!" I yelled, tearing at the fabric. "*Fuck!*"

"That's a good way to ruin a dress," a voice said from behind me, and everything in my stomach and chest collided into a dense ball of iron, and then sunk to my feet, where it threatened to explode.

I wanted to whirl around and scream at him, or reach out and hit him. But then he was kneeling in front of me, his long fingers skillfully unhooking my skirt from its hedge prison.

"What are you doing here?" I challenged.

"Looking for you," he replied honestly, glancing up at me

with those crystalline blue eyes before looking back down to my dress. His palm moved up from my ankle to my calf to support my foot while he extricated the boot. And even through my stockings, I felt the heat of his skin like a brand. Something deep within me tightened and twisted. It was something like lust, but a much, much deeper itch than lust.

Hating my traitorous body's reaction, I abruptly withdrew my leg from his hold. "I thought if I gave you my safe word, you would stop pursuing me," I muttered, more to myself than to him, but he must have heard, because he finished unhooking my skirt and stood up, his expression guarded.

"You're right," he admitted. "But I had to see you one more time. I had to talk to you."

"What could there possibly be to talk about?" I asked, keeping my voice cold to hide the heat that flamed deep in my stomach.

"I saw Mr. Cunningham," he said, and that hateful name was like a bucket of ice water on my desire. I hugged myself and backed up a few steps.

Silas didn't chase me, his features uncharacteristically serious. "We talked about marriage. And Hugh. And he rejected my suit entirely."

"You asked him if you could marry me?" I asked.

"Well, if the board would support my suit for you, yes."

"And this was after you had Mercy Atworth fucking you with her mouth. You still thought you would try to marry me." My voice was flat, and I didn't care. Let him think I was completely unaffected by him. Let him remain oblivious to the turbulent waves of heartache and lust he stirred in me.

"Yes."

"Goddammit," I swore. "Why? Why can't you just leave me alone? Isn't life bad enough without you coming back here and breaking my heart all over again—"

I broke off, suddenly realizing that I'd inadvertently revealed too much, and there was no hope that Silas had missed my slip, because he was now pacing steadily toward me, a dark cast to his face.

"What did you say?" he asked, his long legs covering the distance between us. I felt like a gazelle slowly being circled by a lion.

He thought he could intimidate me? Fuck him. "You heard what I said," I said defiantly.

Something between a growl and a hiss rumbled up from his chest.

"Say your safe word, Molly," he said, coming closer. "Tell me to stop."

God, that face, with that chiseled jaw and those carved cheekbones and the firm, masculine lips that were currently pressed together in determination.

"What are you going to do?" I dared. "Fuck me until I say yes to marrying you? There's not a chance in hell, especially after you and Mercy—"

"*Say. Your. Safe. Word.*" His voice was almost menacing, almost *mean*, and Lord help me, I felt my response to that dampening my thighs.

"No," I said haughtily. "I won't."

He was on me then, his arms like steel bars around my back, pressing me close to him. I was forced to lift my face to see his; he glowered down at me, his eyes like the heart of a flame, hot and blue and deadly. The last time he'd looked at me like this, like he wanted to eat me alive, had been last year...

"Say it," he demanded. "Make me stop."

Was it stubbornness or lust that made me dig in my heels? I wasn't sure. But I could feel his erection grinding into my corseted stomach, feel the possessive way his hands roamed across my back, until he dug his fingers into my hair and forced my head back even farther. My pulse pounded everywhere—my exposed throat, my wrists, my empty, wet cunt.

It pounded for him.

"I'm not saying it," I said. "You can't make me."

"Oh, is that the game?" he growled. "I have to make you?"

He bent his head down and nipped at my throat, and my whole body sang. Sang with righteous fury and pent-up resentment, maybe, but it sang nonetheless, singing for him and him alone. The nip turned fierce—a real bite—and I hissed, raising my hands to shove him away even as my center clenched with want.

He caught my hands before I could push him, and then his mouth was on mine, searing and marking and angry. Why he was angry with me, I didn't know, except that maybe we were always destined to be angry with one another. And then his mouth parted my own with insistent, needy force and his tongue slid against mine, licking and fluttering and plundering my mouth.

My knees seemed unable to hold my weight, and without breaking our kiss, he reached down and hooked his arm behind my legs and I was swept up into his arms. He carried me to a nearby bench and sat down, and for a moment, I felt the twin tugs of desire and disappointment. The kiss was deep and urgent and I never wanted it to end...but I couldn't have *this* with Silas. This greenery and blue sky and this pleasant bench in the cooling shade—this was what lovers did and we were *not* lovers. We were...something else, maybe. But not that.

Then he pulled away and in the space of an instant, I caught his blue eyes, as dark and inscrutable as the midnight sky. And then I was summarily flipped over onto my stomach on his lap, my forearms braced on the bench and my feet hanging off the other end.

"Silas," I protested, struggling, and he pressed a firm hand on the small of my back as the other worked to lift up my skirts. I never wore drawers at the Baron's, and Silas rumbled in approval when he revealed my naked skin. I realized what he was doing a second too late; his palm cracked against my ass with a noise that rang through the maze.

"No!" I shrieked. "Let me go!"

His hand on my back held me tightly in place. "You know what you have to say, Molly. Say it. Say it, and I'll stop."

I froze. Saying it was admitting defeat, and I hated defeat. I liked to win—I *loved* to win, and if Silas thought he could spank the safe word out of me, he was dead wrong. Besides, there was the way that my ass felt after the slap—warm and glowing—and the way my breathing sped up as he shifted under me and the way that my nipples tightened as his fingertips ran lightly over my thighs.

But.

But.

I wasn't used to being spanked. Hell, I wasn't used to being dominated at all, had never let a man run my body this way, not since Mr. Cunningham had bought my virginity from me for a hundred thousand pounds when I was sixteen.

You'd never let a man since Cunningham...until Silas last year.

"Aren't you going to say your word?" he crooned in my ear. "Are you really going to let a man you hate lay you over his lap and spank you?"

I told myself that the shudder my body gave at his words was a shudder of anger and not a shudder of lust. I looked over my shoulder at him. "It doesn't matter how hard you spank me, Silas. You won't win."

Smack.

I cried out as his hand landed on my bare flesh.

Smack.

Smack.

Smack.

Three blows in quick succession, and I was so unused to pain, so unused to being held down. My whole body was squirming now, my face rubbing against my wrists as I fought for the air that had been driven out of my lungs by the pain.

His hand returned to my ass, not to strike, but to rub and caress and soothe. Stupidly, I found myself sighing into his touch, even raising my hips and trying to buck into his hand.

"Greedy girl," he murmured, his fingers dancing past the small crevice that led to my cunt. I whimpered, bucking my hips again. The hand on my back pressed harder and he laughed a low laugh. "Greed becomes you, Mary Margaret."

And then he trailed his hand down to my knee, where he nudged it to the edge of his lap, spreading my thighs and exposing my pussy.

I gasped.

Warm summer air blew over the wet, swollen flesh, teasing and gentle, and I somehow felt more wanton than I'd ever felt. How? In a closed garden with no other people around, with a man who'd seen my cunt a hundred times before? How, when I'd been naked before scores of people, in packed ballrooms and in heated, languorous orgies? How did Silas make me feel with a few spanks and a summer breeze like I was the naughtiest—and also the most desirable—woman to ever walk this earth?

Silas groaned above me. "Fuck, you're so wet, Molly. Please. Say your safe word. If you don't—"

Smack.

I moaned. The pain flamed along my skin for half a second—half an unbearable second—and then dissipated, leaving to resettle deep in my core. I moaned louder as a finger teased about my wet folds.

"It starts with a *c*, doesn't it, Mary?" he asked quietly. "The word?"

The finger moved lower, glancing across my clit, and I inhaled sharply. And then it went back up and, without warning, pressed hard against the pucker there. Resistance and discomfort and the memory of those times *before*—when he'd fucked my ass so hard that I couldn't breathe, when I'd climaxed so long and so hard that I forgot my own name—it was muscle memory that drove my hips up against that thumb and nothing more.

It slid partway inside, and he murmured, "Did you miss this, Mary Margaret?"

"Don't call me that," I ground out, his pressing thumb short-circuiting my thoughts.

"Why not? It's your real name, is it not?"

"Because not even my family used my real name. No one calls me that!"

Smack.

"I call you what I feel like calling you, are we clear on that?" he asked sternly. "You are mine to call what I want."

"No. I'm. Not," I managed.

"Maybe not. So use your safe word to prove it," he goaded. "Use it and I'll stop spanking you. I'll even take my thumb out of your ass."

My hips were now wriggling of their own accord, my ass begging for more punishment, my pussy begging for more pleasure. My nipples pressed hard and tight against my corset.

I didn't want to say my safe word. I wanted him to fuck me.

There. I admitted it to myself.

"I won't say it," I said.

"Fine," he said. "Have it your way."

CHAPTER 7

SILAS

*H*ow dare she say that I had broken her heart again? How dare she finally, *finally*, admit that I affected her, that she cared about me, and then act like it was nothing?

No. It was not nothing.

It was a not-nothing that tore my heart out of my chest and then brought it back to life, it was something that gave me anguished pain and even more anguished hope all at once. If I'd broken her heart again, that meant that she still loved me, which meant that there was a chance I could salvage all this. A chance I could fix everything.

Quickly, without giving her a chance to realize what was happening, I hooked an arm around her waist and picked her up as I stood, her hips on my shoulder and her head hanging down my back and her adorable feet—tiny and encased in expensive white leather—kicking madly in front. I would be lying if I said that this didn't make my already insistent erection even more insistent.

"What are you doing?" she demanded. "Put me down!"

"You know what to say, love," I told her as I carried her toward the maze exit. "You know how to get me to stop."

She fell silent. Predictably.

I grinned, glad she couldn't see it, since it would make her even angrier, but I couldn't help myself. She was so fucking competitive—to the point that she would endure the unendurable from me simply so that I wouldn't win.

Frankly, I didn't want to win. I wanted to fuck her. I wanted to shower her face with kisses and apologies and promises, and I wanted her to accept my proposal and let me be her husband. I would be perfectly happy if I never heard the word *Clare* again, especially not in that strangled, dead voice she'd used at Mercy's house.

So why did I feel compelled to push her? Why did I need to spank her, to force her, to debase her? I'd never needed to do that to a woman. That was Julian's style, not mine; I was the easygoing one, the happy one. But when I saw Molly, when I was with her, something else took over. This disturbing need to have her cries filling the air, her ass glowing pink, her wrists gathered in my hand. Was it because I knew that Molly wouldn't let just any man top her? And that turned dominating her into some kind of prize?

Or was it because, somehow, I knew that she needed it? More than me, even?

We exited the maze, and I carried her to a long stretch of lawn, laying her on the springy grass and kneeling between her legs. Birds trilled around us, butterflies flapped, and in the distance, a fountain trickled a sleepy August trickle. It was the kind of day made for fucking in the grass.

Her head twisted up. "We're too close to the house, someone will see—"

My hand clapped over her mouth, my skin slightly darker and rougher than hers, my fingers pressing into the soft skin of her cheek.

Oh, I liked the way that looked. I liked it very much.

89

"You let me worry about that. Or say your safe word. But if you're not going to say your safe word, then you'd best say nothing at all."

I let my hand fall from her mouth as I rucked up her skirt.

"And why is that?" she asked, her eyes glowing a furious blue. "I'll talk when I damn well please, and just because I haven't said my safe word doesn't mean I won't say anything else..." Her voice trailed off as the skirts reached her waist, baring her wet, swollen pussy to me.

I took a finger and rubbed her clit—once, twice, three times. Her eyes fluttered closed.

I pulled my finger away and she groaned. "I think you'll play by my rules," I said, "if you want to come."

"That's not fair," she said, eyes still closed.

Smack.

This time I slapped the inside of her thigh, the fiery red imprints of my fingers appearing almost instantly on her milky white skin. She drew in a sharp breath through her teeth but didn't cry out, letting her legs fall open as I returned my attention to her clit.

"I decide what's fair right now, do you hear me?" I slapped her other thigh, and then—just once and only a little hard—I slapped her pussy, my dick surging as I did it.

God, when did I turn so diabolical?

Her back arched and she did cry out this time, and I wished I could bottle that cry and then uncork it on lonely nights. I slapped her pussy again and then immediately sealed my mouth over hers, swallowing the breath she gasped out, swallowing the soft shriek she gave.

She moaned underneath me, her legs wrapping around my waist and pulling me down so that my hips settled between her legs. Her heels dug into my back and her hands were everywhere, and now she was trying to flip us over, so that I would be on the bottom and she on top, a position we'd fucked in so many times that I'd lost count. But I wasn't having that today, and so I reached up and found her throat with one hand, wrapping my fingers around her neck. I gave a light, experimental squeeze.

She stilled, her lips parted slightly.

I reached down with my other hand and found her cunt, slick and ready for me. "You get so wet when I wrap my fingers around your throat," I whispered as I slowly unbuttoned my trousers. "You want me to fuck you like this, doll? You want to come with my hand on your neck?"

She stared right into my eyes. And nodded.

I took in a breath, the full force of the moment hitting me all at once—my hand strong and rough around her throat, her bared legs and bared pussy, her asking for me to screw her while I nearly choked her...

Fuck me. If I had thought that having Molly O'Flaherty riding me was the most alluring thing I'd ever seen, I now knew better. *This* was the most alluring, the most tempting, to the point where I was worried about coming before I even finished pulling myself out of my pants.

Finally, my trousers were undone, and I fisted my erection, giving it a few mindless pumps while I stared down into Molly's face. She had features like a china doll, delicate and pale and feminine. And the dusting of freckles across her nose and the pink blush in her cheeks made her look like the girl I'd met ten years ago in Europe, brash and bossy and carefree.

She wasn't carefree now—I could see the worry lines in her forehead, the exhaustion in her eyes. I vowed to myself that I would make her forget, just for a few moments, everything except us, everything except joy and pleasure and what it felt like to be loved.

"Silas," she murmured, squirming underneath me. "Please."

"Well, since you asked so nicely, Mary Margaret..."

I brushed the flared tip of my cock against her, loving the way she shivered as I did, loving how hot her flesh was, how wet. I leaned over to get a better angle, shifting some of my weight onto the hand around her throat. The skin there was thin and smooth, and underneath, I could feel the tiny, butterfly-like beats of her pulse. Her life, her entire life, was under my hand. For the first time, I really understood how much stronger I was than her, how much bigger. Even if she tried to fight me off, even if she wanted me to stop, I could hold her down and do whatever I liked, use her however I wanted.

Perversely, that realization made me even more intent on loving her, on protecting her. The rest of the world saw Molly as strong and capable, but I knew that deep down, she needed to be taken care of and cherished and worshipped and petted—not left alone to suffer and endure. She needed someone she could let down her guard with, someone who could help her find peace and calm in the middle of her chaotic world.

I wanted to be that someone, even if for only for a few moments.

My cock pressed against her entrance, her flesh parting as I pushed, until the head of my dick was buried. I braced my weight on my other hand and let up on the pressure on her throat, and then slowly slid in farther, hissing out a low breath as she took me in.

"So tight," I groaned quietly. "So fucking tight."

And then I slid in the rest of the way, buried to the root. I paused. Not because I wanted to draw out the moment for effect or because I wanted to give her time to adjust, but because I wanted to savor it. Savor her. I hadn't been inside her for so many months.

"You feel perfect," I told her. "You feel so fucking perfect. Your pussy was made for me, you know that? It was made for me to fuck." I pulled out and thrust back in, and her back arched off the ground again. "Doesn't that feel good? Doesn't that feel so good?"

"So good," she echoed, her hips wriggling in an effort to rub her clit against me. "So...*oh.*" I changed my angle and buried myself deeper, making sure that the base of my cock ground against her as I did.

"You like that?" I asked, leaning down so that my mouth was at her ear. I continued to thrust and grind, deep and hard and slow, the way women like it, pressing on her throat just enough that she was reminded of my hand there, of my strength and power over her. "You like it when I fuck you like this? How about when I fuck your ass? Do you remember how hard you'd come then?"

She nodded, her eyes closing, a flush creeping up her neck. She was getting close. And as much as I wanted to go over the edge with her, I wanted to watch her. I wanted to watch her come undone under my body, I wanted to watch her unravel and fall apart and drop her steely-strong mask, just for me. Only for me.

I pushed in and pressed down and squeezed, grinding and rubbing, and her mouth was open in a breathless moan and her eyes were pinned to mine, and then I released my grip on her throat. Her climax took her, seized her, tossing her about like a rag doll as the convulsions wracked through her. I could tell that she couldn't breathe, hadn't been able to catch her breath after I let go and her orgasm snatched her up, and so I watched her carefully as she finally came down, gulping in deep, desperate breaths.

"Oh my God," she finally wheezed. "Oh my God, that was so good. That was…" She reached up and pressed a palm against my cheek. Her gaze was open and vulnerable. "Only you," she finished, in a voice that was somehow both less and more than a whisper. "Only you make me feel like this."

"I know," I growled. "Because you're mine."

Something in her expression shuttered, and I frowned, but she wrapped her hands around my neck and pulled me close. "Come inside me, Silas," she murmured. "I want to feel it."

So I obeyed, my arms sliding around her back to cradle her as I thrust into her, burying my face into her neck and smelling the sweet, cinnamon smell of her skin. She was so beautiful and so perfect and I wanted to be like this forever, smelling her and feeling that tight silk grip around my cock forever. I wanted her to be my wife.

She said my name again, and that, along with the thought of her as my wife, did me in. It sent heat curling down my spine and into my cock, tightening and tensing until I was rutting mindlessly, groaning as it finally crashed over me, through me. I pulsed long jets of cum deep into her, so deep that that I could feel my hips digging into her inner thighs and my balls pressed against her ass. I dropped my head beside hers, my forehead resting on the grass, loving the feel of her body so slender and soft under mine, wishing I could keep her gathered in my arms forever.

After a minute or two, I withdrew and raised up onto my knees to look at her. Tousled red hair and rumpled silk skirts and her cunt still open to me. I used my thumb to open her to my gaze, wanting to beat my chest like a fucking caveman when I saw the glistening traces of my semen.

I bent forward and kissed her clit, gently and reverently, and then I layered worshipful kisses on the insides of her thighs, above the lines of her stockings.

"Marry me," I said in between kisses. "Have my children. Be mine."

She sighed, her body twitching with a suppressed giggle when I reached the back of her knee. I showed her no mercy then, nibbling and licking through the thin silk of her stockings, and fending off her arms as she sat up and tried to push me away from the ticklish skin. I tackled her back down, transferring all those nibbles and licks to her ear and her jaw and her lips, until her giggles turned into quiet moans, happy sounding inhales of surprise whenever I found a particularly sensitive spot.

"What do you say?" I asked, pausing my work to look down at her. "To marrying me?"

"Silas…" she said, trailing off. "We can't. Besides…"

"Besides what, doll? Besides the fact that I love you?"

She met my eyes, and her gaze was sharp, perceptive. "No,

Silas. I didn't mean that. I meant that you fucked Mercy—and you almost did it again—and I don't think I can forgive you for that."

Pain lanced through my chest. "Please tell me that's not true," I whispered. "Please tell me there is a way I can win your forgiveness."

She struggled to sit up, and I let her, even though what I really wanted to do was pin her to the ground and kiss her until she relented. But I knew I didn't deserve that right, I hadn't earned it. It didn't matter if I fucked Molly a thousand times, it was her mind and her heart that I wanted to possess, and so it was pointless to keep her here if she didn't want to be kept.

"The truth is that I understand why you did it," she said, now avoiding my eyes. "And maybe it could have been me who ruined it given enough time, maybe it *would* have been me, because we're so much the same, Silas. And we weren't made for marrying or for children or for love. We enjoy fucking, we're good at fucking, we're both good with money and business— that is what we must content ourselves with."

"I don't want to be content with that," I told her. "I want more. I want you."

She stood up, arranging her skirts so that they hung straight down to the ground and when I reached out to help, she took a step farther back. "What I'm saying is that even though I can trust you with my body, I know I can't trust you with my heart." She studied the ground, as if it held all the answers, but even from this angle, I could glimpse the shine in her eyes. "I shouldn't have done this…this was a mistake."

I scrambled to my feet, panic clawing at the base of my skull. I couldn't lose her; she couldn't walk away, not after what we had just shared.

"Molly…"

"I'm not going to say the safe word, Silas. I don't need a safe word for a game I'm not playing."

I drew in a ragged breath. *Please play*, I wanted to beg her. *Please let me at least try to win you back.*

She extended her hand, like she wanted me to shake it, but instead I took it in my own and kissed it, letting my lips linger there. Goose bumps raced up her arms, and when I straightened, a single tear had spilled out of her eye, falling slowly down one cheek. She let me pull her closer, and I wiped the tear away. "Don't do this," I said. "Don't let Hugh win…don't let the *board* win."

She shook her head. "*I* am going to win, Silas. You think just because I let you spank me, I'm submissive? When have I ever been anything other than the mistress of my own life and the mistress of everyone around me? I control my life, I control what happens from here on out, and you aren't man enough to wrestle the reins from me, so just give up."

And with that, she was out of my arms and walking away, leaving me with her tears drying on my finger and a broken heart.

CHAPTER 8

SILAS

 wo weeks later

Miss Molly O'Flaherty of London and Mr. Hugh Calvert, Viscount Beaumont, request the pleasure of your company two weeks hence, August the Thirtieth, to celebrate their engagement...

I STARED down at the invitation in my hand. A thick cream-colored card, bordered with gold, embossed with looping letters and bearing the seal of the Beaumont family at the bottom. I tossed it away without bothering to look at the location or the time; it did not matter where the party was to be held. Even if it was held in my own bedroom, I would not attend, I could not. For the sake of my own sanity, if not for the sake of propriety.

It had been two weeks since that terrible afternoon on the Baron's lawn. I'd tried writing Molly, calling at her house, haunting the hallways of the Baron's mansion...and all to no avail. She would not see me, she would not answer my letters and I knew she was deliberately abstaining from her usual parties and circles to avoid me. And of course, I had heard about her engagement, rumored to have been settled on the very evening we'd parted ways. She'd agreed to marry Hugh with my seed still dripping down her thighs, and I didn't know if that made me furious, depressed, or hysterical with laughter.

All three, really, depending on the day.

The envelope for the invitation caught my eye, and I examined the back of it. *To Silas*, it said, in the sharply elegant handwriting that I recognized as Molly's. And below it, several tiny dots of ink, as if she had set her pen down several times to write something else, but had stopped herself before the words could come out. Instead, it only read, *Deepest regards, Molly*, at the bottom.

Cold words. Polite words. I crumpled the paper in my fist and then went in search of a drink.

"So will you go?"

The Baron and I were atop two of his finest horses, riding around his expansive property. I suppose I must have struck him as disconsolate and listless (and frankly pathetic) when he'd walked into his library to find me slouched on a sofa with a bottle of gin, and so he'd suggested we go for a ride. Predictably, I'd confessed all the things that had happened between Molly and me since I came back to England.

I watched a flock of birds fly up from the leafy stand of trees near the white gravel path leading out from the stables. "How can I?" I finally answered, not bothering to keep the bitterness out of my voice. "It would hardly be appropriate."

The Baron shrugged. "I don't see how it could be *in*appropriate. Several of Molly's ex-lovers will be there, myself included.

Even Julian and his wife are coming into town for the event." I could feel him looking at me as I turned my horse slightly to the side. "Are you sure that it's not your jealousy preventing you from going?"

"Of course it's my jealousy. And my broken heart. And the fact that I hate Hugh, and I hate that she's been forced into this ridiculous marriage."

"Hugh has been friends with us a long time, if only on the periphery. Surely if Molly wants to be with other men during their marriage, he'll allow it, especially given that their marriage will be one of convenience."

The Baron sounded so calm, so sure. And it was easy to believe, if only for a minute, that I could still be with Molly as a lover, even after her marriage. "But I don't want that," I admitted. "I want her all to myself."

"How interesting, then, that you haven't, in turn, given all of yourself to Molly." The Baron raised an eyebrow and kicked his heels, urging his horse forward.

I followed, feeling a bit sullen, like a child who'd been called out on his mischief, but then the Baron turned around, so that our horses faced each other and we could look eye to eye. "Silas, you know how deeply I care about you. Like a brother. And I love Molly too. I would hate to see the beautiful friendship you've cultivated over the years dissolve."

I hung my head. "I know. I should be the bigger man here and gracefully accept my defeat. Hugh won. Mr. Cunningham won. I lost."

"Cunningham?" the Baron asked. "Who's that?"

I reached for the flask of gin inside my jacket pocket and helped myself to a healthy drink before answering. "Frederick Cunningham is the informal leader of her company's board. He is the one who insisted that Hugh be Molly's husband and refused to accept any bribe I could give him."

"Interesting," the Baron mused. We started riding again as the

Baron pondered…whatever it was that he was pondering. After a few minutes, he said, "I'm sorry for my silence. I just didn't realize Hugh's cousin was involved in this."

Hugh's cousin.

Cunningham.

I stopped my horse. "What?"

"Yes," the Baron said, stopping as well, and there was a small frown on his lips. "There was a scandal a few years back—a girl was appallingly abused at The Corinthian. A man had paid an exceptionally high price to take her virginity, and when the madam had found the girl the next morning, she'd been beaten and sodomized." The Baron's hands tightened on his reins. "She was not yet seventeen."

"Christ," I muttered.

"The man was Frederick Cunningham."

I suspected as much, but the confirmation infuriated me. That stupid mustache and the ridiculous mincing way he drank his wine…all that time, I'd been sitting across the table from a rapist and I'd had no idea. I wanted to ride to wherever he was right now and beat his face in. I wanted to watch his body bob in the Thames.

The Baron looked equally furious as he recalled the incident, and a furious Castor Gravendon was a terrifying thing, an avenging god straight from Roman myth, muscled and hulking and implacable. Castor may have been a dominant man, but he had no tolerance for cruelty.

We nudged our horses forward in silence, each of us wrapped up in our individual fantasies of retribution.

"As you might know, The Corinthian leases its property from me," the Baron continued after we turned a corner near the woods, calmer now. "The madam approached me for help—she had no recourse to seek justice for this girl, but she wanted to make sure that this man couldn't hurt another in this manner again. My circle is wide and varied and well-connected to many high-end establishments like The Corinthian, so I spread the word about him. Mr. Cunningham was barred from the best of the London brothels and has since had to travel overseas to find what he craves."

"What an abominable pile of shit."

The Baron nodded in agreement. "And when, in the course of spreading this word, I discovered through mutual friends that Frederick Cunningham was actually Frederick *Beaumont* Cunningham, Hugh came to me and asked that I keep their relation quiet. I granted his request, since I could understand why Hugh wouldn't want to be associated with such reprehensible behavior."

I thought of my suspicions in the Cafe Royal. "So that must be why Cunningham was so set on Hugh marrying Molly. They're family."

"Possibly. And as I understand it, Hugh has been living off loans from Cunningham for quite some time."

"But Hugh's a viscount," I protested. "I thought surely he must have plenty of money…"

"There are many peers of the realm who aren't more than paupers, Silas. Hugh is one of them."

I sat back in my saddle and thought. I had at least believed that Hugh was marrying Molly out of some misguided affection or love, that he wasn't using her for money, but that didn't seem to be the case. And for Cunningham, using Hugh to marry Molly must have been a convenient way to infuse his relative with cash, while also solidifying his control over Molly. Any children she bore would be Beaumonts and related to him.

The realization made me so miserably angry that I had to close my eyes for a minute and concentrate on breathing normally.

"I'll see if I can find anything more," the Baron said. "I hate the idea of Molly being tied to that man, in whatever way."

"Me too," I agreed.

Me too.

"Does Molly know?" I asked. "About Hugh and Cunningham?"

"Surely she must," the Baron said.

But I worried that she didn't. And she deserved to know. But how did one tell somebody something this crucial when they refused to see you? "She won't believe me if I tell her," I said with a sigh. "Because she'll think I'm interfering out of jealousy, not concern."

"Which you are," the Baron pointed out.

"Both. It's both."

He accepted that and we rode back to the stables, dismounting the horses and passing the gin back and forth for a few minutes. From here, I could see the lawn where we'd made love, where I'd parted her folds to see my seed inside of her. My cock twitched at the same time my heart twisted.

I don't need a safe word for a game I'm not playing.

"Do you think Molly is really a Dominant?" I asked, knowing the question probably seemed abrupt and irrelevant to Castor and also not caring.

He looked taken aback. "Our Molly? Certainly not."

That surprised me. "You don't think so?" But then I remembered that, even though it had been years ago, Molly and Castor had played together. "Was she submissive for you?"

Castor took another deep draught of the gin. "Yes and no. Yes, she submitted physically, which for her is a tremendous step, but she never submitted to me mentally or emotionally. She never found the submission fulfilling, but it wasn't because of the submission itself, I think. I believe Molly needs to have complete trust and love in the person she's submitting to, and while she trusted me, she didn't love me. Which is why we never played together more than two or three times—it wasn't rewarding for either of us."

I thought about this.

"Just because a person refuses to be topped by unworthy men doesn't necessarily make her dominant," Castor added. "No more than your allowing a woman to take charge in bed out of politeness or laziness makes you a submissive." He gave me a pointed look. "For her, she's never found a man worth that surrender. And you've never found a woman worth exerting that level of effort for."

"I want to believe that. I want to believe that I can be the kind of man who can take care of her, but…"

"But it feels like she won't let you?" the Baron finished for me.

"Right."

"Silas," the Baron said, screwing the cap back on the flask and handing it to me, "spanking her in a maze once isn't enough to make her forget the ways that you've hurt her. If you want her to surrender to you, if you want her to allow herself to be brought under your care so you can love and protect her in all the ways she needs and deserves it…then you are going to have to surrender yourself to her first."

∼

MOLLY

Hugh wanted to honeymoon in Paris.

I didn't want to honeymoon at all.

After all, a honeymoon was a celebration, and what was there to celebrate? Certainly not our marriage, which would be a sham. Certainly not our happy future, because there wouldn't be one. And certainly not the possibility of a family, which I mulled over as I drank my morning tea in bed—the same tea I drank every morning, a brew I'd learned from my auntie in Ellis before we'd moved to Liverpool.

"What the Pope doesn't know…" she'd said with a wink, as she'd showed me the dried bundles of herbs hanging from her ceiling. I'd been ten when she'd taught me how to brew the tea, and I didn't really understand until I was older what a gift she had given me. I'd been able to live my life as freely as I wanted, and even now that I was being chained to a man I didn't love, I still wouldn't have to bear him any children if I didn't want to.

But I could have happily had children with Silas...

I finished the tea, refusing to let that thought settle. No, it was done and over. I would save my company now and worry about the rest later, and so what if my chest felt as if someone had cracked it open and scorched the inside? So much the better. Hope couldn't grow on scorched ground, and hope was for the foolish.

If anything, this would make me stronger.

Not for the first time, I thought about leaving London and going back to Ireland. Finding some quiet stone cottage by the sea and drinking whiskey all day. A place where money and businesses didn't matter, where I could be free of any consideration aside from what I wanted. Silas could be there. It could be the two of us, secluded and spoiled, spending every moment with one another. And I would watch him staring at the surf, watch the way the corners of his eyes would crinkle as he squinted into the setting sun. I would watch those long, strong hands flex and curl as he sifted through pebbles on the beach.

But all of that only made me remember the last man I'd been on an Irish beach with. My father, walking home from my mother's funeral, him telling me about opportunities for dockworkers in Liverpool...

Daddy.

I slid off the bed and went in search of a dressing gown, trying to avoid the crushing wave of sadness that came when I thought about my family. My mom, dying of consumption just months after my little brother. My father, moving us to Liverpool and then to London, working his way up from dockworker to manager and then to the owner of his own company, only to succumb to the same disease as my mother before I turned twenty-one.

He had poured all of himself into his work, and it was his blood and sweat that had created O'Flaherty Shipping Lines.

Well, his blood and sweat and one very lucky investment.

It had been my sixteenth birthday. We had just moved to London, and my father had taken all the money he'd earned in the last two years and purchased one ship—a beaten-up, decades-old vessel called the *Aquamarine* (which he'd promptly renamed the *Clare*, after our home.) My father was a prompt deliverer and fairly priced, and before long, we had more work than the *Clare* could handle. Then came the *Shannon*, named for my mother, the *Sean*, for my brother, and finally the *Molly*. We had the beginnings of a fleet, the makings of a thriving business.

Since my father had made sure I'd been schooled, I was far better at the accounting and bookkeeping than he was, and so I'd spent every evening after school and every Saturday in our warehouse, working the numbers.

Mr. Cunningham had come into the warehouse we rented in the East End, looking for my father, but upon seeing me scribbling at a desk, had sauntered over with a smile. He'd been a young man then, newly married. He was the handsomest man I'd ever seen, and I had looked up into his face and been temporarily paralyzed by the sudden awareness of his *maleness*, or rather, of my *femaleness*. He'd looked at me like I was a woman, not a girl. And I had felt very compelled to tell him, when he'd asked me if I was Aiden O'Flaherty's daughter, that yes I was, and that I had also just turned sixteen years old.

"What a special age," he'd murmured. "Happy birthday, Miss O'Flaherty." And then he'd presented me with the small daffodil from his buttonhole. I'd clutched it while he'd spoken with my father about the possibility of investing. Only my father and I knew how desperately we needed the money—we were swamped with work and if we didn't purchase new ships, we would have to start turning away orders. When he'd left, he'd placed a small card on the desk where I worked. Even I, as inexperienced as I was, could tell the card was expensively made, with its thick stock and filigreed letters, and so I didn't dare refuse the order dashed in ink on the back.

See me.

And below that, an address in Knightsbridge.

The next day, when my father thought I was at home, I went to Frederick Cunningham's house. Looking back, I cannot believe that I went...sixteen years old in a new city, going unchaperoned to a strange man's house. I'd always been bold, but this had been outright dangerous. I suppose I'd felt special, somehow, with my card and my wilting daffodil. And when I was admitted into the palatial townhouse, I felt a little bit like a princess from a fairytale. That ended quickly, however, when I'd been shown into his library. There'd been none of the charm of the day before, none of the smiles. He'd made me stand before him as he fired question after question at me. What was the net worth of the shipping company? How many men did we employ and what did we pay them? How quickly could we recoup the cost of a new ship? The kinds of questions that he'd asked my father, but he must have sensed I'd have better answers for him, given that I actually kept the books of the business.

"What would you do with an investment of a hundred thousand pounds?" he'd asked finally, lighting a cigarette.

I'd blinked in the smoke. *A hundred thousand pounds...*I couldn't even fathom that amount of money. I stammered around possibilities of more ships, more men, advance payments on tariffs, layering it with copious *thank yous*, until he'd held up a hand to forestall me.

"Don't thank me so soon. I haven't given you the money yet, Miss O'Flaherty. It must be earned."

"Earned?" I'd had enough sense then to start feeling wary, although I hadn't had enough sense to run home to my father.

"Yes," he said, and now his smile was back as he leaned forward, his eyes gleaming through the smoke. "Earned by you."

In the end, I'd made the decision as I made most of my decisions—brashly and without much thought. What was my virginity worth to me? I'd seen dairy maids in County Clare tumble in barn lofts at my age; prostitutes in Liverpool younger than me, letting unwashed old men between their legs for a single coin. And a hundred thousand pounds was a princely sum for what amounted to a small barrier of flesh...

I'd gone the next day to be examined by Cunningham's physician, who'd ensured that I was indeed a virgin, and then I was deposited at a gentleman's club not far away from his house.

It had not been quick. It had not been gentle. He'd wanted more as soon as he'd finished, and he went over and over again, my blood and his cum the lubricant after my own body had run dry. He'd slapped me, bruised me, and called me awful names. But even the pain and degradation I could handle. I'd refused to cry, forced myself to remain strong, for the company and for my own sense of pride. I had gotten myself into this situation...and I would see myself out, with as much dignity as I could muster.

But in the end, as he was fucking me one last time, he'd looked down at me and at my distant expression, and his face turned calculating. "No, my dear," he'd said. "You don't get to pretend me away."

I hadn't understood what he meant at first, and even as he pulled out and knelt between my legs, I still hadn't understood. It wasn't until he wiped me with a clean linen cloth and then lowered his face to the battered parts in between my legs that I realized what he was doing.

"No," I'd whispered, trying to roll or buck away, but his hands—sharp with their vain, long fingernails—dug into my hips and kept me pinned to the spot. The true horror of it unfolded over the course of the following days and years, but even then, I could grasp an inkling of this terrible act. Of his tongue lapping and licking, of my body responding, of the way my mind screamed *no* as my body climbed inexorably towards climax.

He'd made me come.

He'd made me enjoy it.

And with that manipulative little act, he made me feel equally complicit in his perversion. The first man ever to give me an orgasm was the man who cruelly bartered for my virginity and won. It was the man who shoved his cock back into me as soon as my orgasm started, so that I was forced to feel the unfamiliar waves of pleasure while he was inside me and looming over me.

It had taken me years to get over that. Years to find the joy in sex, although God knew I tried very, very hard and very, very often. In fact, it wasn't until I met Julian and Silas in Amsterdam that I succeeded, realizing that if I had control of the situation— if I could be on top, or at least direct my own orgasm, then I could enjoy it without reservation. I'd slowly but surely won back my sexuality from Cunningham, although there were still so many dark corners of my memory where he lurked, so many places where fear and pain dwelt.

Except with Silas. When he'd spanked me in the maze, when he'd hoisted me over his shoulder and carried me out to the lawn to ravish me, like a brute in some Italian opera, and *oh God*, when his hand was wrapped around my throat...

I shivered at the delicious memory.

Somehow, when Silas was That Silas, that predatory Silas I'd never seen before last year, somehow he drove all the other darknesses away. There was only room for him, for his Cambridge-accented voice delivering those filthy commands, for his hands gripping my neck, for his dick, hard as steel and so delightfully thick and long. He could do the exact same things Cunningham had done, and I would welcome them gladly because when Silas used me, it was with boundless respect and affection and *love*, and because I wanted him to.

Not that the difference mattered. Not anymore. I had no choice but to marry Hugh, no matter how much I longed for Silas.

I stared at my face in the mirror. Drawn and fatigued. Wary and sad. What would it look like if I were wearing Silas's ring on my finger? Would I still be drinking that tea every morning?

I shook my head to clear the thoughts and got dressed for the day, mechanically pulling on my clothes and trying not to cry. I'd received word that van der Sant would be in town tomorrow and there were a few last minute things I wanted to check before he arrived. My business still had a future...even if I didn't.

CHAPTER 9

SILAS

*J*ulian, Ivy, and George were staying with Castor, so I invited myself to stay as well, mostly to be close to my good friend, but also on the remote, slim, nigh-impossible chance that Molly might come to the mansion. I didn't know what I would do if I actually saw her—I only knew that something needed to be done. I loved her. I wanted to take care of her. But my past failings prevented me from doing just that, and I didn't know where to go from here, how to escape this net we'd woven around ourselves.

George and I were lying together on the plush Persian rug in one of the scores of receiving rooms that the Baron seemed to have. George, almost five months old, had sat up for a little while, before rolling onto his back and beginning to industri-ously gnaw on his feet. Ivy sat pensively in a window seat, a book half-open on her lap as she stared into the gardens, prob-ably wishing she could escape outdoors. And Julian sat near me, reading a paper, patiently waiting for me to divulge all of the reasons I was a pouting, pitiful lump.

"You do realize I can wait all day?" Julian asked dryly, not bothering to look up from his paper.

"I'm busy," I said, helping George grab his other foot. I wasn't really though, and it wasn't even that Ivy was in the room—we'd been together, quite intimately, on the couple of occasions that Julian had wanted to share her with me, and I tended not to be shy around women after I'd come in their mouths. No, it was simply that saying all of the words out loud—*all of them*, including the ones about how I'd fucked up totally with Mercy— was too damn hard. They lodged in my throat, along with all the guilt and pain and misery.

But later, after supper, when Ivy had taken George up to bed, Julian and I were back in the library with tumblers of the Baron's best gin, it all came pouring out. How I'd come to England after getting Julian's letter. How I'd found Molly and made my proposition, only to find myself with Mercy the very next morning. I'd told him about the sex on the Baron's lawn and Molly's subsequent engagement to Hugh. About Cunningham.

By the end of my story, true darkness had settled outside and a servant had come in to light a small fire to ward off the slight chill creeping in from the windows.

"I never liked Hugh," Julian remarked, taking a sip of gin. "He always struck me as a voyeur of sorts. But I wouldn't have suspected him of conspiring with someone to take advantage of Molly."

"I know! The only reason we allowed him in was because of Molly, because *she* liked him."

Julian tapped his fingers on the glass. "So does Molly know about the connection between her board and her future husband?"

I shook my head. "And I don't see how I can tell her without her thinking that I'm trying to stir up trouble."

"I'll tell her the next opportunity I have," Julian said without hesitation. "As I am the only one of her friends that has been in an unhappy marriage before, I feel as if I have no choice. She should know everything before she goes to the altar."

I didn't say anything for a few moments, because what I wanted to say was so petulant and selfish that even I recognized how immature I was being. But it pushed itself out of me anyway. "What if you tell her about Hugh and Cunningham, and she doesn't care? What if she still decides to marry Hugh?"

Julian took a thoughtful drink.

When he didn't answer for a few moments, I sighed and set my glass down. "And don't judge me. I know you are wondering whether I'm asking this out of a pure and loving concern for her well-being or whether I'm asking because I'm jealous, and what I want to know is why can't it be both? Why can't I be certain that she'll be unhappy with Hugh and want to protect her from that, when at the same time I want to have her for my own? Why must it be mutually exclusive?"

"I would never tell you that it has to be," he replied slowly. "In fact, I would trust you less if you told me you had no personal stake in Molly's happiness. But you know that Molly won't be steered—not after she's set her course and especially not by a man who's hurt her. And I think that if you don't want her to marry Hugh, then you're going to have to do a whole hell of a lot more than fuck her."

"The Baron said as much," I said glumly, picking up my glass and draining the last of my gin. "But what do I do?"

We sat in silence for a while, the fire popping and the sound of a piano trickling in from some unknown room. I thought of that day a year ago, when I found her crying in her parlor. I thought of my contingency plans. I thought of all the miserable lonely years that awaited me if I let her slip through my fingers. A plan started to formulate in my mind, a plan as distant and frail as those piano notes, a plan that wasn't exactly playing fair. But then again, I'd warned her I wouldn't play fair.

It would take time. Another week, if not two.

"Julian," I said, turning to my oldest friend in the world. "If I told you I wanted to do something a little...*mad*...would you help me do it?"

MOLLY

I was signing off on a few papers before I met van der Sant's delegation at the docks when Hugh set a pile of papers in front of me and then sat down in the chair across my desk, leaning back in a smug pose that unaccountably irritated me.

"What's this?"

The morning sunlight streamed through the windows of my small townhouse library, illuminating the gold in his hair, just like it had Mr. Cunningham's. I swallowed back the bitter taste that always came with memories of that vile man and tried to focus on Hugh's answer.

"...a marriage contract," he was saying. "Very standard, of course, dictating that all of your assets will be conferred upon me at the time of our union."

It was standard, but I didn't bother to hide my frown as I flipped through the pages. I'd known, in a cerebral sort of way, that my money and the company would legally and technically belong to Hugh in the eyes of the law, but I had comforted myself with the fact that Hugh had told me when I agreed to marry him that the company would still be mine in the practical sense. Now, looking at the actual clauses in stark black and white, the reality of it hit me hard. Everything I'd worked so hard to build and protect would belong to someone else. Be possessed by someone else.

"I will have my solicitor look it over," I said. I meant to push the papers away, not wanting to deal with it right now, but a word caught my eye.

Infidelity.

I glanced up at Hugh and then looked back down to the page.

"'In the event that the wife is found to be unfaithful, her husband may be allowed to divorce her and keep all remaining monies, properties and investments...'" I read aloud. I stopped. "Hugh. Explain this."

Hugh shrugged. "It's simple enough. If you fuck someone else, I will divorce you and keep the company." The words pierced me like a bullet. Another reality I hadn't considered—that my sexual freedom would also be at an end.

My hands shook. "Are you serious? You expect me to fuck only you?" I quickly scanned the rest of the pages, finding nothing about *his* fidelity being required. Of course. I had just assumed...I mean, Hugh was part of the same circle I was. For years, we'd fucked whom we wanted, when we wanted, laughing at all the conventional people with their stodgy, sexless marriages. How could he do such an about-face? "Hugh, the things we've done...I thought certainly you were more enlightened than this!"

"That was play, Molly. This is real life now. If I have a wife, she must be faithful to me. I cannot compromise on that."

"And you?" I demanded. "Are you going to be faithful to me?"

"Molly, be serious, please," Hugh said in a pained voice. "Men naturally have excessive desires that have to be sated, but for a woman...I mean, obviously, we have to make sure that any children you bear are mine and no one else's. A woman's fidelity is crucial to the family, and I knew being stripped of your company altogether would be a reliable incentive."

My hands shook. "Are you really threatening me with that? You would leave me with nothing? Without the only *fucking reason I'm doing this in the first place?*" I stood so fast that the papers fell off the desk, scattering across the floor. I didn't care. I leaned forward, bracing my hands on my desk. "Go fuck yourself, Hugh."

"Okay, but..." Again in the pained voice, as if he had no more control over this than I did. "It's either marry me and remain connected to your company, or refuse to marry me and lose it right now."

"I—" I couldn't finish my sentence. There was a ball in my throat, a painful teary ball that made it hard to speak, hard to breathe. All I could see was red and my fingers itched with the urge to claw his face. He must have seen my temper building because he got to his feet and walked towards me, hands outstretched as if approaching a dangerous animal.

"Molly, these are just the formalities, believe me. After we're married, you can continue running the company as you like, no matter what this contract says. And yes, we need to make sure any children are mine and mine alone, but you've always liked sex with me, haven't you? And we can have as much sex as you'd like."

He was very close to me now and he took my trembling hands in his. "Haven't I been your loyal friend all this time? Through all your troubles? I care so very deeply about you, and I want what's best for you. *This* is what's best for you. *I'm* what's best for you."

The anger hovered, just out of reach, like a mirage that refused to resolve into reality. I couldn't hold on to it, I couldn't give it voice, but it was there still, distracting me, making me wary. "I just don't know if I can be happy like this, Hugh," I said honestly. "I'm sorry, but that's the truth."

Hugh looked at me with his deep brown eyes. He *was* very handsome and he *had* been a very loyal friend. A woman could do worse and I knew many women who had. "Would you be more unhappy with me...or without the company you love so dearly?" he asked. "I will do anything in my power to make you happy, so long as it's within the bounds of reason."

That is the difference between him and Silas, I thought. *Silas would have thrown himself at my feet, would have forsworn all reason, and made a ridiculous but gallant fool of himself in the process.*

Silas. I supposed I would never know what he would and wouldn't do for me.

"I will sign it," I said, pulling away from Hugh. "But for the company. Only for the company."

Hugh smiled a smile that didn't reach his eyes. "That's good enough for me."

～

MARTJIN VAN DER SANT was a short man, with thin white hair cropped close around his ears and a precisely trimmed mustache. Even his clothing looked as if it had been folded and pressed with a ruler in hand. He did not smile, nor did he talk very often, but when he did, it was with a clipped Dutch accent that left no room for argument. My encounter with Hugh and his contract had left me shaken, but I swallowed everything down and mustered my most professional, competent demeanor as the other board members and I met van der Sant's party down at the docks.

A man as wealthy and powerful as van der Sant could have easily sent representatives to investigate our assets. The fact that he traveled all the way here to see them for himself told me a lot, told me that he was a man to be both respected and feared. I was proud of the way I ran my company and I knew he wouldn't find anything on the company's end that would dissuade him from partnering with us, but I was more than a little nervous that word of my personal life might reach his ears. I glanced over at Cunningham as we walked along the docks. He was talking seriously with one of the other businessmen van der Sant had brought along, and there was nothing in his demeanor to suggest he was planting rumors about me.

He wouldn't, I decided. He wanted this business deal as much as I did—maybe more than I did. Even he wouldn't jeopardize the chance at more money simply to spite me. Besides, he had taken care to mention my engagement to Mr. van der Sant when we'd introduced ourselves earlier, probably to portray me as a normal, moral young woman.

The dock and warehouse visits went very well, and I was beginning to feel more settled about Hugh and the contract when we escorted Mr. van der Sant back to my townhouse for a late luncheon. "I hope you don't mind if my daughter joins us," Mr. van der Sant said. "This is her first visit to London and she is very excited."

"Of course," I said, sending word to one of my people to arrange for her to be picked up at their hotel.

But when she walked through the doorway an hour later, my stomach sickened. She was not, as I presumed from van der Sant's age, a married woman in her thirties or forties, but a girl. A girl of about fifteen or sixteen, with flaxen blonde hair and gray eyes and a sweet, innocent face. "Everyone," Mr. van der Sant said, "this is Birgit, my daughter."

Birgit made a shallow curtsey, and I knew without looking that Cunningham's eyes were pinned on the girl. I knew he was watching her, observing her sweetly uncertain mannerisms as her father introduced her to the other people present.

I prefer my women fresher...younger.

He wouldn't, I thought for the second time that day, but I was not so certain this time, because Cunningham's eyes still hadn't left the girl and his expression was hungry, like a fox watching a rabbit bounce by. No, even he wouldn't be that foolish. That reckless. Cunningham loved money, and van der Sant was a fount of money. He wouldn't throw that chance away simply to pursue this girl, no matter how pretty and youthful she was.

I saw the way his lips lingered on the back of her hand as he kissed it, and then he did something that nearly made me bolt across the room and shove him away. He handed Birgit the flower from his buttonhole. A daffodil. Her father seemed completely oblivious to her pinking cheeks and fast-fluttering eyelashes, to Mr. Cunningham's entirely-too-assiduous attentions.

And so after dinner, I asked Mr. van der Sant if it would be okay if Birgit and I retired to the parlor while the men enjoyed some brandy and smoking and business-talk. I could tell that my decorous femininity pleased him, but that's not why I was doing this. As soon as Birgit and I went into the parlor, I closed the door and locked it and turned to face her.

She was so sweet-looking. I had looked like that, I knew...I still had men remark on how young and girlish I seemed. Maybe that's why Cunningham still bothered me.

I sighed. "Sit, please, Miss van der Sant."

She sat, looking a bit confused. I sat as well, on the sofa next to her so I could speak softly, hating that I was about to insinuate something so ugly to a girl so gentle and young. But I could not entertain the alternative, and I didn't care if it might somehow circle back to Cunningham, if it would somehow tarnish my own place within the company. Right now only one thing mattered, and that was making sure Birgit stayed safe.

"Miss van der Sant, I'd like to ask you—privately—to do me a favor."

She was clearly still confused, but nevertheless, she drew up, looking eager to please. "Of course! Is it about Father's business here? I would very much like to help."

I saw so much of myself in this girl. And her eagerness only made me more certain that I needed to do this. "I would like you to consider me a friend," I told her, "a confidant. And the things we discuss will only remain between us, so I do not want you to worry that I will speak to your father about any of the things we discuss." *Unless I need to,* I added to myself silently. But I didn't say it aloud; it was more important to cultivate her trust at the moment.

She nodded, her eyes wide.

"That gentleman in the dining room? Mr. Cunningham? I am going to tell you a story about him, and then after I tell it to you, I need you to promise me that you'll let me know the minute he ever tries to talk to you alone..."

CHAPTER 10

MOLLY

*T*he carriage ride to the Baron's the next night was long and uncomfortable. The Baron was hosting a party in honor of Julian and Ivy's visit, and Hugh had forced himself along. He had also taken the trouble to remind me that although we were only engaged, he'd still prefer it if I didn't sleep with anyone tonight. The way he'd said *prefer* made it clear that all of his other threats held true in this case as well. In yet another unexpected corner, I was forced to sacrifice happiness for the hope of holding on to my company.

"But I will make you come plenty, if you'd like," Hugh had offered once we got in the carriage. He'd tried to slide over to my seat, but I claimed a headache, and he sulked back to his side.

A headache. Jesus, Mary and Joseph, but I hated myself. I'd become one of those terrible women who avoided sex on pitiful pretexts, who lied instead of just saying *no* in plain language. But I was becoming increasingly aware that I had very little power in this dynamic between Hugh and me. Not if I wanted to keep my company. And so I had to placate him, which for now meant lying, but later it might mean actually having sex with him, and that made me very unhappy. It shouldn't—he had never been a poor lover and he was so good-looking, but...well, if I was being completely honest with myself, I only wanted Silas right now. The only tears I wanted to cry were tears drawn forth by my smarting ass as he spanked me...the only hands I wanted to feel around my waist were his wide ones.

That's enough, I told myself firmly. I was a big girl. I needed to accept my fate and move on. Just like I had with Cunningham all those years ago—I was doing what I had to for what I wanted, which was my company. I could handle a loveless marriage. I could handle a life without Silas. I could handle anything as long as I had my company and my dignity.

I sat up straighter in the seat. I was Molly O'Flaherty, dammit. And I would sacrifice anything for what I wanted.

And I would do it without complaint.

My mind flitted briefly to Birgit van der Sant safely ensconced in her hotel with her papa. I sincerely hoped that a different future awaited her.

The Baron hosted many parties, large and small, lavish and quiet, and this was somewhere in between. Despite being something of a recluse, Julian had many old friends in London, and there were even more people curious about the new Mrs. Markham, the mysterious beauty that most of the town had heard about but only a few had seen. And tonight she did look radiant, if a little reluctant to release her chubby boy into the capable arms of the nursemaid. But Julian leaned over and whispered something to her, and she finally relinquished the baby with a kiss and a quiet admonition to the nurse to come fetch her at the slightest hint of fussiness.

Watching this exchange from my seat on a nearby sofa, my stomach clenched. Not out of jealousy—although there was still the lingering version of Molly that remembered fancying herself in love with Julian—but out of a mixed sense of fear and regret. I never wanted to be Ivy—I didn't want to be the woman unable to enjoy her dinner because her baby was a room away. But when I looked up and met Silas's eyes across the room, there was this moment, this stupid moment, where I wondered what it would be like handing off a little blue-eyed child, with its father whispering in my ear that it would be okay.

I looked away quickly, my cheeks burning. I couldn't afford thoughts like that. Not anymore.

I'd made my decision.

The one real blessing of the night was that Mercy wasn't there, a fact Hugh seemed irritated about, even after the Baron claimed he'd invited her and there must have been some sort of mistake in the delivery of the invitation. He said this with a completely impassive expression, with complete authority, even though we all knew Mercy's absence had been deliberate.

"Thank you," I whispered to Castor as we walked into the dining room to eat, and he reached over and squeezed my hand before handing me into my seat. Sitting here with Silas while I had Hugh's ring on my finger was terrible enough, but if I'd been forced to looked at Mercy's sleek hair and pouting lips the whole night on top of that, I would have died of fury and humiliation. Perhaps that was why Hugh was disappointed, perhaps he wanted that reminder of Silas's failings near at hand tonight, to remind me that he was still my best option.

Dinner was served, the Baron engaged in quiet conversation with Ivy about her aunt, Silas and Julian talked about some new railroad line coming though Yorkshire, and Hugh's arm draped possessively across the back of my chair. Chatter from the other guests and music from a small band in the adjoining room filled the air, so nobody noticed my uncharacteristic silence, which I used to watch Silas. Now that I knew, beyond a shadow of a doubt, that I could never be with him again, it changed things. Softened things. I could look at him without my mind crowding with memories of him and Mercy, and for the first time in a long time, I could just *see* him. His jaw, clean-shaven and slightly pointed; his sparkling eyes; the way he smiled as he listened to

Julian talk—smiled with his eyebrows lifted expectantly, as if he was genuinely excited to hear what his friend had to say. That was Silas, really: simply *happy*—happy to be talking, happy to be drinking, happy there would be dancing later. He lived in the moment, for the moment, and never had it felt more so than when the moment had also contained me. Why had I never noticed before? Why hadn't I appreciated that when it was mine to appreciate, for however short a time?

As if he felt me watching him, he glanced over at me, stopping my heart with that smile and those dimples, with the way his smile faded into something hungrier. Slowly, he licked his bottom lip, his eyes moving from my face down to the bodice of my gold silk dress, where the tops of my corseted breasts rose into round swells. He shifted in his seat, not bothering to hide the fact that he was adjusting himself.

Hugh noticed and cleared his throat, his hand moving from the back of my chair to my shoulder. I wanted to shrug him off, I wanted to continue staring at Silas, but I didn't dare. There was too much at stake. I glanced down at my lap, where my hands rested, trying to focus on the contrast between my skin and the gleaming silk. On the still-unfamiliar diamond ring on my left hand.

But Silas didn't look away from me; I could feel the heat of his stare even across the table. "Castor," he said, "didn't you say there would be dancing?"

"Of course," the Baron said. "After dessert."

"Good," Silas said, and that was it, but I still kept my head down all throughout the meal, answering Hugh in monosyllables and ignoring everyone else. I knew that if I spoke too much or looked up, my face and voice would betray the heat nestled inside my chest. The raw longing. Because the last time we were together here at the Baron's…

Greed becomes you, Mary Margaret...

I decide what's fair right now, do you hear me?

So tight.

So fucking tight.

I coughed, my face burning, my whole body hot and clenching at the memory of him fucking me, as if a red-hot chain had been wound around my cunt and then wrapped around my chest.

"Are you okay?" Hugh asked, an eyebrow raised, and I nodded, sliding my chair back.

"Just a little overheated," I murmured. "Excuse me." And I hurried out of the room, taking care not to glimpse Silas's face as I did.

∽

SILAS

Molly fairly ran from the room in a rustle of silk and elaborately curled hair, and after she left, I found Hugh looking at me—staring me down. I gave him a small shrug, as if to say *I was over here the whole time, I had nothing to do with it*, even though we both knew the last part wasn't entirely true. Whatever Molly had been thinking over there, her cheeks growing pink and her breathing growing fast, I would have bet the entire Coke estate that it had to do with me.

And Hugh knew it.

I flashed him my widest, happiest grin. He looked away, his jaw clenched tight.

That's right, I thought. *Be jealous. Because you'll never truly have her, even if you manipulate her into marrying you.*

Dinner concluded without further incident, and we moved into the ballroom, where drinks were already circulating and music was playing. I danced with Ivy first, sweeping her away from Julian with a laugh and spinning her into the lively waltz the band had struck up.

Ivy's hand was firm and warm around the back of my neck and her dark eyes were friendly, if a little feral.

"The last time you had your hand on my neck like this, buttercup, I do believe my face was between your legs," I commented.

"I don't remember hearing any complaints at the time," she remarked.

I grinned. "No, you didn't. I was quite happy to be there. I don't suppose there's any chance that you and Julian would like an encore performance?" I meant it in jest...mostly. I wanted to stay dedicated to Molly, but even the most dedicated man couldn't refuse his best friend, right?

She laughed dismissively, but a telling blush bloomed on her cheeks. "I thought perhaps you would be spending the night with Molly."

My grin faltered. "I believe she's taking her engagement to Hugh rather seriously."

Ivy looked at me with a concerned expression. "And how are you feeling about that?"

Terrible. Shitty. Like my life is over.

"I have everything well in hand," I said instead, twirling her so fast that her skirts billowed out around her legs. "I have a plan." I didn't mention that it was a terrible plan which essentially had no hope of working, because Julian would probably tell her that himself at some point, and also because Molly walked into the ballroom just then, and my world shrank down to a vision of gold and scarlet, silk and hair, and nothing else could exist.

"Go to her," Ivy whispered in my ear. "Before Hugh does."

It wasn't very gallant to end my dance with Ivy early, but it was unthinkable not to go to Molly, and so I led Ivy off the floor as graciously as I could, and since Hugh was occupied in a dance with another woman, I strode over to Molly and took her hand without asking, tugging her onto the floor.

"Silas," she said, her eyes darting around, looking for Hugh. "We can't—"

"Even the strictest etiquettes allow for an engaged woman to dance, Molly, and this is hardly a house of etiquette. And besides, how can Hugh complain about us dancing while we are both in plain sight of him? We could hardly get away with anything with him so close." I cinched an arm around her waist, pulling her body flush against mine while I leaned down to murmur in her ear. "Although, I'd like to try."

"Silas..." her voice wavered, and there was that flush of red on her chest, like she was burning up from the inside. Blood went straight to my groin as I fantasized about pressing my body against her flaming skin, as I remembered how hot her ass was, hot and tighter than the tightest fist.

We moved to the music, stepping easily around each other, moving in perfect time to the music. Molly was a fantastic dancer and I liked to think I was not so bad myself, and I could feel the eyes of the room following us as we moved. I knew we must cut a captivating picture—Molly and her gleaming gold skirts and her red curls piled high and spilling over one shoulder, me and my perfectly tailored tuxedo and my wide hands guiding Molly expertly through the steps.

Molly wouldn't look at me, however, keeping her face turned to the side, exposing the delicate line of her jaw to me. I wanted to bite it.

"Silas," she said as we danced. "Hugh has...he is...he's threatened to take the company away from me."

I kept perfect, easy rhythm and I didn't let my face betray the sudden flare of fury I felt, but I let my voice carry my displeasure with this revelation. "Explain. Please."

And she did—telling me about the contract, about Hugh's ultimatum, his demand that her fidelity start now. It explained so much about her behavior tonight, so much more timid and passive than I was used to from her, and it also explained why Hugh seemed to be so singularly possessive at dinner.

"You can't be thinking of signing this contract, Molly," I told her. We spun and came back to center, my hand finding the small of her waist again. I heroically resisted the urge to play with the laces and buttons there.

"What choice do I have?" she asked impatiently. "If I refuse, I get nothing."

"Legally, you would technically get nothing either way. What if you marry Hugh and he reneges on his verbal agreement with you to allow you access to the company? What if you end up with nothing *and* married to him?"

A small line appeared between her eyebrows. I wanted to bite that too. "Hugh wouldn't do that," she said.

"Are you sure?"

She didn't answer right away, but when she did, her voice was so heartbreakingly tired. "What's my alternative, Silas? Walk away from it all? This company that my father built, that *I* built?"

"Is it worth your future? Your happiness?"

"I don't need to be happy," she said firmly. "I just need O'Flaherty Shipping to thrive."

I spoke with my lips close to her cheek, and she shivered as my breath skated over the delicate skin there. "Ask me for help, Mary Margaret. Ask me."

"There's nothing to be done."

"There's always something."

She looked up at me, her blue eyes glittering in the light of the chandeliers. "Not this time."

I hoped she was wrong. I hoped that my unhinged plan would work, and I almost told her about it, right then and there. But it depended completely on secrecy, and I didn't want Hugh to get even an inkling of what I was doing, and a change in Molly's attitude towards everything might signal to him that something was off. Not to mention that I couldn't bear to let her down—what if I told her and then I ended up failing?

No, silence was better for now. But I hated that defeated look on her face, the rigid way she held her body, as if already preparing for the onslaught of misery her choices would unleash upon her. I couldn't comfort her the way I wanted, with my lips and my hands and my cock, not with Hugh here. But maybe I could comfort her with my words and say all the things I needed her to hear right now.

"Do you want to know why I fucked Mercy?" I asked.

Her already tense body stiffened and she tried to pull away, but I didn't let her. My hand tightened around hers, and the other tightened against her waist. "Don't do this," she said, angry and frail all at once.

"Yes, Mary Margaret, we are doing this and you are going to listen to me." My voice left no room for question, and her lips parted ever so slightly.

She liked that voice.

We whirled past another couple and then I started talking again. "That day," I said, knowing I wouldn't have to clarify which day I meant. It would always be *That Day* for us, that defining and pivotal moment where everything had shifted from almost unbearable joy to unbearable pain. "That day, we woke up in bed together, and I looked at you...your body tangled in the sheets, your hair still knotted from the night before, and then you woke up and do you remember what happened?"

"You took me on a picnic," she said quietly.

"We didn't fuck, we didn't fool around. I took you out in the sunshine, and I kissed you on that blanket for hours. Just kissed. Do you remember?"

"Yes, Silas," she said, and she looked up to me. Her pulse pounded in her throat, her pupils wide and dilated. "I remember."

"Kissing you is heaven," I told her. "Your mouth is perfect, you know that? And Christ, I could have kept kissing you until the stars came out. But we were coming here, to the Baron's for a party, and you needed to change into an evening dress and I needed to change into my tuxedo. So we went our separate ways. And it was on my lonely ride to the Baron's that I panicked. Was I arriving at Castor's a single man? Or was I now attached to you? And if so, it was the first time I had been anything other than unattached, and that was terrifying. That's not who we were, Molly, not who we *are*. We fuck people. Lots of people. We don't go into the sunshine and kiss for hours, we fuck and we move on, and what was happening to me? Who was I, if I wasn't acting like the man I'd always been?"

We spun again, and she swallowed, but she didn't say anything, her rapt expression encouraging me to continue.

"And so I got to the Baron's already panicked, panicked but still desperately in love, and then I saw you and Gideon dancing already, and he leaned down and kissed you. Kissed that mouth like it wasn't the same mouth I'd spent hours laying claim to just that afternoon, and you let him. You let him kiss you."

Her face went white. "Silas…"

I gave a curt shake of my head to let her know she wasn't allowed to speak yet. "You pushed him away, I know. I saw. But you hesitated before you did, and I thought to myself, *what if she's right to hesitate?* What if we were making a mistake trying to bring this new thing between us into our old world? What if we were denying who we really were? And then Mercy was there, beckoning me upstairs, and I had to prove to myself that I didn't care that you kissed Gideon. That I wouldn't care if you went to bed with him. I had to prove that this meant nothing, because if it didn't mean *nothing* then it would mean *everything*, and God, Molly, I was terrified of that. Terrified like a sinner about to convert. Terrified like a man about die and go to heaven, because the reward was paradise but the price…the price was me. My life. My soul. It would no longer belong to me alone."

I took a deep breath and said what I should have said nine months ago. "I loved you and I betrayed you. I indulged the weakest, basest parts of me, I was selfish and despicable and disgusting. I was low. I *am* low. I don't ever deserve your forgiveness, and I won't presume to ask for it, but you deserve my groveling and my apology and so here it is. I am so sorry that it hurts. I am so sorry that when I look in the mirror at myself, all I feel is hatred. I am so sorry that sometimes I can't sleep, and

I pace the room and drink and cry until I'm so drunk and emotionally exhausted that I can't remember why I started drinking in the first place.

"I am so sorry, and there's nothing you could command me to do right now that I wouldn't do, because you deserve that. You deserve my blood and my pain and my torture. You deserve to watch me branded with hot iron, and I would do it gladly, if only to spend that much more time with you."

The music swelled and came to an end, but I didn't let go of my partner, not caring that it was my second breach of etiquette that night, not caring that Hugh was surely glowering somewhere in the margins of the ballroom. Let him seethe, let him rage—he wouldn't come out here to claim Molly, not tonight, because it would make him look weak. Even he knew that.

Instead, I kept hold of her until the next waltz began, watching her face. She had turned away from me again, allowing me to see the exquisite quivering in her lower lip, the rapid sweep of her long eyelashes as she tried to keep her tears to herself. I wanted to lean in and blot them away from her lashes with my lips, I wanted to kiss away every tremor in her chin and throat, and I fucking couldn't. And I wanted to ask her what she was thinking, if she was crying out of rage or hurt or understanding or *what*, but I also knew she wouldn't want to break down in front of everybody here, and I worried that interrogating her as to her feelings would push her closer to the edge... but fuck, I was desperate to know. Was I making everything worse by being honest?

No, I decided. It was time for honesty.

"Let me tell you what should have happened that night. What I wanted to happen, what I spend every night falling asleep wishing had happened," I said, guiding her easily through the steps of the dance. Even looking away, even about to cry, her dancing was still flawless, her body still perfectly in tune with mine. This time, as my hand tightened against her waist, I did allow one finger to play with the laces there, tugging hard enough that she could feel it.

She blinked faster.

"I wish we had kept kissing in the park that day. I wish that I had pulled back and looked at your sweet face and had the courage to admit to myself that I didn't want to see anybody else. I didn't want to share my time with anybody else. I wanted only *you*, and there was no way in hell that I was going to go to a dinner party when the only place we belonged was in a bed together, just you and me."

A tear finally slipped past her eyelashes, spilling gracefully. And then another and another, and I could feel her ribs seize and stutter under my hands as her breathing turned jagged.

"I should have taken you out of that park and back to your bed, and then I should have spent hours with my face between your legs, fucking you with my mouth until you couldn't speak or think or even breathe, and then I should have asked you to marry me. Not because of your company or because I wanted a family, but because I wanted you. Because I wanted to spend every night of the rest of my life with you underneath me, every day counting the freckles on your stomach when we woke up."

She was crying in earnest now, her face crumpled and her voice thick. "But why?" she asked. "Why did you love me?"

I moved my hand from her back to her delicate jaw, taking it in my fingers and tilting her face to mine.

I stared directly down into her eyes as I talked, feeling the words burning everywhere—my heart and my mind and my stomach. "Why *do* I love you, you mean. I love you right now, still...and more than ever. And it's because you provoke me, because you provoke everyone. Because you're strong and because you need someone you can be frail with...because you're the smartest woman I know and sometimes also the stupidest, because you're honest and determined and sometimes manipulative. Because I want to see Ireland with you, because I want to see everywhere with you, and I want you to read me novels in the evening with your adorable lilt, and I want you to let me hold you when it's all too much. Because I've known you for ten years, and it feels so desperately like no time at all, and I need more."

I finally stopped talking, my own breathing coming fast now, my own tears close at hand. I felt suddenly naked, raw, like my skin had been flayed from my body, my rib cage cracked open and my beating heart exposed for all to see.

Molly's dancing slowed until we both stood stock still, our hands clasped and her eyes pinned to mine, and despite the tears, her eyes had grown unreadable, hard-shelled like jewels.

"Say something," I begged. "Please. Anything at all—tell me I'm an ass for saying this, a prick for still chasing after you when you're engaged, a monster to beg for forgiveness. Tell me to get ready for the hot irons. I don't care, just please speak."

The other dancers moved awkwardly around us, and in the corner of my eye, I could see Hugh finally pushing his way toward us, his patience exhausted or his dignity overridden by his irritation, one of the two.

Molly took a deep shuddering breath and then straightened her shoulders. "Yes, Silas, you are an ass. And a prick. And a monster. And you are something worse than all of those things put together."

My voice was hoarse. "Which is?"

"Too fucking late."

CHAPTER 11

MOLLY

*W*ho could sleep after that?

Not me.

I'd left Silas on the ballroom floor, looking wrecked, those eyebrows lifted ever so slightly, like a puppy who'd been kicked and didn't know why. But those eyes, bloodshot and glossy and still that evocative China blue—those eyes knew everything, understood everything.

I'd left the Baron's, fending off Hugh with a continuation of the headache excuse and came straight home to collapse on my bed in a puddle of silk and tears. I had no way to process any of the things Silas had said...not the apology, not his explanation of what had happened that night between him and Mercy...

I rolled over onto my side, blinking sightlessly at the small white fireplace across the room. I'd completely forgotten that Gideon had kissed me that night. It had been so casual, such a common occurrence in my life, that at the time, it had taken me a moment to realize why I was unhappy with it. It had taken me a moment to realize that I'd grown accustomed, in the space of only a few days, to having only Silas's lips on mine, and I didn't *want* anybody else's, and so I'd politely pushed Gideon away. And Gideon had been more than a gentleman about it. But if I had been Silas, watching from the margin...yes. I could understand. The shock and the fear and the desperate need to prove that it didn't matter, because if it did matter, then everything had to change.

And neither of us was ready for that last year.

You deserve to watch me branded with hot iron, and I would do it gladly, if only to spend that much more time with you.

I sat up and hugged my knees to my chest, the ball gown scrunching and bunching around my legs, and I knew I should call in my maid to help me undress. I knew I should simply go to sleep, because I had chosen my path, and what did it matter that the man I wanted had laid his heart bare to me tonight? That he had given me the messy totality of him, his failings and his fears, along with all of his reckless, foolhardy pledges of atonement and his fervent adorations? Every part of it was real and raw and just so gutting to witness because there was no veneer, no shield —and Silas had always been a man of veneer. A man of smiles and politeness and charm, where you sensed that unknowable thoughts flickered in the blue depths of his eyes, but knew you could never learn them.

Except I could learn them, I had learned them, because he had given them to me, along with his heart.

And I wanted to give him everything of mine in return. I'd told him it was too fucking late for a happy ending for us, and it was. But maybe it wasn't too late for something else.

It doesn't matter, Molly, a sensible part of me thought. *Go to sleep.*

Instead I slid off the bed and took a lamp off my end table. Padding downstairs, I went to my office, the soft rustling of my skirt unnaturally loud in the empty house. I went to my desk, where I found Hugh's contract. I flipped through the pages until I found what I was looking for:

Infidelity, which shall be defined as the following acts...

I glanced up at the clock. A little before midnight. It would take me at least thirty minutes to get back to Gravendon Manor, and possibly another thirty to find the other thing I would need to do this...oh my God, was I really thinking about doing this?

I glanced down at the contract, at my hand with its diamond glittering in the lamplight.

Yes. Fuck it all, I was doing this.

SILAS

After drinking what felt like a gallon of gin, I went to bed before midnight, which was practically unheard of for me, but I was exhausted. Not necessarily my body, but my mind—my thoughts were a grayscape of rejection and defeat, and I couldn't even pretend to feel otherwise. I excused myself to Castor, Julian, and Ivy and then went up to my room, where I shucked my clothes and toppled face first onto the bed, waiting to die. I would just lay here and refuse to eat and drink, and then I would die, and at least that would be better than knowing what it looked like to have Molly O'Flaherty walking away from me after I'd offered up everything.

Yes, that was the plan. I would consign myself to death, and then everyone would feel terrible—especially Molly—and she would weep at my graveside, and then somewhere, from Hell or Heaven, wherever I ended up, I would at least have that satisfaction. Castor would shake his head sternly and Ivy and Julian would name their next child after me, and poets would write lyric odes to my steadfast dedication to love.

All this decided upon, I promptly fell asleep.

When I woke up, I had that heavy, groggy disorientation that comes with having slept either too much or too little. I was unable to tell if I'd been asleep for days or only for a few minutes, although the lamplight I was currently squinting against indicated it was still nighttime. I started to roll over to shutter the lamp, only to find myself impeded in some way that my sleep-fogged mind didn't comprehend. The impediment turned out to be silk ropes, binding my wrists and ankles and securing them to the posts of the bedstead.

"They're tied pretty well. In case you were thinking of struggling," a voice observed.

I blinked once, hard, to clear my vision. "*Castor?*" What the fuck?

The Baron just smiled. He was sitting in an armchair by my bed, a book open on his lap. I glanced around—soft lamps, silk ropes, me still stark naked from when I'd undressed earlier. Was he planning what I thought he was planning? I'd been with a couple of men before, but never in the receptive capacity, and I wasn't sure that drunk and heartbroken was the way I wanted to rectify that.

"Relax, Silas. I'm only here to be a witness."

My brow furrowed. "A witness to *what?*"

He nodded towards the door, which had just clicked open, revealing a slender young woman in her middle twenties, a woman I recognized from a few of the parties at the Baron's but whose name I didn't know. She was as naked as I was, small-waisted and small-breasted. More arresting to me than her nudity was her dark red hair, unbound and tumbling down her back. If you had only seen Molly a handful of times, it would be easy to confuse the two, although this woman had brown eyes and no freckles and a very timid expression you'd never see on Molly's face.

But that didn't matter right now, because the only thing that mattered was that this woman was naked and walking towards me, and that I was naked and tied to a bed, and *no fucking way* could I stomach the idea of sex with a stranger right now. I yanked on the ties again, this time in earnest, growing more panicked as the Baron's words proved true and the ropes refused to give.

"Castor, untie me," I pleaded.

My loyal ally these many years, the man Julian and I saw as a mentor, shook his head.

"You are not my friend anymore," I said, my voice tight as I tried to kick at the leg ties.

The Baron let out a loud laugh. "It's for the best, Silas, I promise."

The woman approached the bed and stood at the side, looking at me almost shyly. This gave me hope. If she was shy, then she might be nervous. If she was nervous, then maybe I could talk her into turning her pert little ass around and leaving the room. Leaving my bereaved heart and my soulless body alone. "Look," I told her. "I don't know what you've heard about me, but it's not true. I mean, it *was* true, but it's not true right now. Or any more. I don't want to have sex with you—I'm sure you're a very nice person and you are very pretty, but I only want one person right now, and you're not her. I'm sorry, but that's how it is."

She cocked her head to the side, and then someone stepped out from behind the screen in the corner of the room.

Molly.

"Silas, I'm flattered," she said with a small smile.

I sucked in a breath. "Jesus, Molly."

She moved over to the bed, on the opposite side of her would-be doppelgänger, and everything about her was designed to send tendrils of heat through me. Jolting my heart awake and—more embarrassingly given my utter and complete nakedness—jolting my dick awake. She wore a dressing gown the same golden color of her dress earlier tonight, her furled nipples tight and hard under the thin silk. Her thick hair tangled and waved around her shoulders, hanging down to her waist in a mass of glorious copper. Somehow, the mere suggestion of her naked form under that silk did far more for me than the overtly naked girl perched just on the other side of the bed.

"Come here," I said, before I could stop myself. Before I could think about the painful way we parted, before I could think about her vengeful fiancé and his ridiculous contract. Before I could think about the other people in the room. I just wanted her close. I wanted her touching me, her cinnamon smell surrounding me, her hair tickling my face and chest.

She didn't climb onto the bed with me, but instead raised her hand and ran her fingers from my wrist down to my chest, where she splayed her hand against my pectoral muscle. The warm pressure of her touch sent more blood to my groin, and now my desire was completely and utterly apparent.

But I didn't care. I didn't give a fuck about anybody else in this room. I kept my gaze on my Molly.

"Come here," I repeated.

She bit her lip. "I want to," she whispered.

"But," Castor interjected, standing from his chair, "we have a slightly unusual arrangement tonight."

Molly nodded and her face cleared, as if the Baron's voice had reminded her of something crucial. "What you said to me tonight…" She glanced up at Castor and the woman, and then back down to me, her expression uncomfortable. Molly didn't like emotions and even less liked feeling them in front of other people. "I reacted poorly. And I want you to know what it meant to me, all the things you said…all the things you made me feel."

"And this is how you wanted to show me?" I couldn't help it —despite everything, I grinned. I mean, I was willing to forget all the heartache of tonight, if it ended where it looked like it was going to end. But then I remembered. "But what about Hugh? And the contract?"

She sighed. "Exactly." Her fingers trailed down my chest to the ridges on my stomach, back and forth, back and forth, until she reached my navel. I hissed and my erection bobbed to full strength. But her hand went no farther. "I can't show you the way I want to show you. But I looked at the contract, and there is a way around it." She moved her hand from my stomach and I exhaled with disappointment. But then her hand was caressing my cheek and I turned into her touch.

"Castor is acting as a legal witness, because Hugh wouldn't dare to contradict the word of another peer in court," Molly continued. "And Viola is going to help us."

"Help with what—*shit*." A hot mouth closed over my cock, small and wet, and all I could see was that red hair moving over my pelvis. I tried to squirm away, and when that didn't work, I tried to buck away, groaning in frustration and something worse.

"Shh," Molly said, and she pressed her fingers against my lips. I stilled, but I didn't shush.

"Molly, please don't do this to me," I beseeched her. "I fucking love you. I don't want anyone else. Please don't—*dammit*." Viola had reached between my legs and was now gently toying with my balls. I was doing everything I could not to enjoy it, not to feel it; I thought the coldest, driest, dullest thoughts I could think of. I thought of Molly's face when she'd walked in on Mercy and me, I thought of hearing her say *Clare*.

"Clare," I said hopefully. "Clare?"

"Nice try," she said and then she shoved her fingers in my mouth. *Shit*. That was hot.

"Just listen for a minute," she said seriously, or at least as seriously as one can say something when one is shoving one's fingers down someone's throat. "I want to fuck you. I can't. I want to suck you. I can't. I can't touch your cock, and a man definitely cannot touch any part of me 'with intent to bring to satisfaction.' But the contract says nothing about witnessing you perform sexual acts with someone else. It says nothing about me touching myself while you watch. And so here's what's going to happen tonight. You are going to do as I say, you are going to take what I want to give you and take it when I want to give it to you."

"It's adorable when you get bossy," I told her when her fingers slid out of my mouth to stroke my stomach. But adorable or not, I didn't like this. Or I didn't *want* to like it. "Molly, we don't need someone else to do this. We can still share something without touching, we don't need someone to be your proxy, and *shit shit shit.*" Viola had just sucked one of my balls into her mouth. My arms strained against the ties while I struggled to regain focus, all while Molly looked down at the scene happening around my groin with frank lust and undisguised longing, *which was not helping.* "I don't want to hurt you again," I managed, after a minute. "I don't want you ever to doubt that you are the only one I want."

It was a ridiculous statement to say when a woman was actively tonguing every crease and seam of my balls, but I meant it. My eyes met with Molly's, and I tried to pour every ounce of feeling and truth into my gaze. "Please," I told her. "Don't make me do this, when all I want to do is spend the rest of my life making everything else I've done up to you."

Molly sat on the bed, facing me, her robe pulling slightly to the side as she did, exposing her freckled collarbone at the same moment Viola's tongue darted someplace unusual and amazing. I groaned.

Molly made a little purring noise at the sound of my groan, looking over her shoulder to see what Viola was doing. She looked back at me with a smile. "Silas, don't you see? This is completely different than what happened with Mercy. I'm here with you."

She leaned forward, putting her hand on the side of my cheek, her hair tickling my chest and face the way I had fantasized about earlier. "You and me, it's not the exclusivity we need. It's the connection. As long as we're doing something together, it's still about us. It's still *for* us. As long as we're together, we are *sharing* something. And I want to share this with you tonight."

"But we can do other things…"

Molly was already shaking her head, standing up and

unbelting her robe. "I don't want other things. I want this. I want it messy. I want it memorable."

Castor cleared his throat from the other side of the bed. I'd completely forgotten he was there. "I will make sure there are no legal ramifications. Molly assures you that there will be no negative emotional ramifications. If I were in your position, Silas, I would stop protesting and enjoy what these two women want to give you." He arched an eyebrow at me and then sat back down. He didn't pick up his book, however, merely leaned back and braced his head against his fingers, as if waiting for the show to begin.

I turned my gaze back to Molly, and she bent over my face again, only the barest sliver of space between our mouths, her breath warm against my lips. I tried to rise up to kiss her, but she pulled away, laughing. I watched as she reached up and guided one ivory shoulder out of her robe and then the other, holding the fabric to her chest for a moment, until she let it slide from her arms and drop to the floor.

I caught my breath, my already stone-hard cock now painfully stiff. I hadn't seen Molly naked since last year, and the sight was arresting. Her pert breasts heaved with each breath, the planes of her body slender and smooth and sprinkled liberally with freckles. I watched the muscles move under her taut stomach as she came back to the bed, and then my attention was stolen by the way her tits swung as she crawled next me. I wasn't sure what I expected her to do then, but it wasn't lay beside me, resting her head on my chest, as if we were about to snuggle ourselves to sleep.

But of course, Molly had nothing sleep-related in mind.

"Move back up to his shaft," Molly ordered Viola, and I could feel Molly's voice tickling under my skin as she spoke with her head against me, the vibrations moving through my chest like a cat's purr.

Viola obeyed, her mouth tracing a wide, hot line from my root to the blunt cap of my dick.

"Lick his tip," Molly breathed, and we both watched as Viola did, her tongue flickering across the slit at the top. I let loose a ragged breath, and Molly tilted her head to look up at me. "Does it feel good?"

I hesitated. Should I lie and say no? Was I supposed to be reluctant to enjoy this? Because mostly I was, but also Viola had reintroduced her nimble fingers to the equation, and God, they were everywhere, digging into my thighs and cradling my balls and caressing my perineum, while her tongue still swirled around my crown.

"Answer me," Molly said, reaching up to touch my lips. "Because if she's not doing a good enough job, I'll have to give her a little encouragement."

"I—" Wait, was that supposed to be a bad thing? It was so hard to think like this.

My silence was apparently enough of an answer for Molly, and she got to her feet and walked around the bed to a place behind Viola. I missed the compact warmth of her body, but my pouting ended quickly as Molly cocked her hand and slapped Viola hard on the ass. The woman yelped and then redoubled her efforts on my dick, circling my shaft with her fingers while she sucked on my crown.

"*Christ.*"

"Is she doing better?" Molly demanded, one red eyebrow arched. She causally rubbed the spot on her friend that she'd just smacked, waiting for my answer.

"I—yes. Yes, it feels good."

Molly's fingers ran over Viola's back and the other woman shivered, goose bumps pebbling everywhere on her fair, freckle-free skin. She guided Viola to shift on the bed so that Viola knelt facing away from me, and then when she bent down to resume her worshipful adoration of my dick, I was treated to the soft lips of her cunt and the small, pink pucker above that.

I closed my eyes. Old Silas would have loved this. Old Silas had spent many nights with multiple women in various configurations, nights with one woman perched happily on his face while another perched happily...elsewhere. But New Silas wanted something different, New Silas wanted Molly and only Molly.

And it was so fucking unfair that Molly was doing this to me, making me respond to another woman when I only wanted her.

"Open your eyes," Molly ordered. I did, keeping my gaze well away from Viola, and having something of a realization at the same time.

"Next time we do this," I told Molly, "you're going to be the one tied up. Next time we do this, I'm going to make you submit to whatever I want, even if it's another man fucking you. What do you think about that?"

She didn't answer, but the pink flush in her cheeks and the part of her lips betrayed her response.

I continued, "You're doing this to stay in control, and it's not going to work."

"I'm doing this because of the contract," Molly maintained.

"No, you're doing this because if my hands were free, if it was just you and me in here, you know you wouldn't leave this room as the same person. You know that nothing would be the same, and you can't let go of that feeling of security and sameness right now, because everything else is so uncertain, everything else is changing, and your sense of self is all you have left."

"Listen to him," Castor said from his chair. "I think he's right."

Molly shook her head. "This isn't about control, Silas."

"Maybe not," I conceded. "But maybe it is. Maybe, in spite of tying me up and watching another woman fuck me, you are still going to leave here changed. You are still going to leave here completely wrecked, thinking of me and of the effect I have on you, knowing that you can't live without me."

She leaned closer to me. "Is that a dare?"

"Are you scared that I'll win?"

She rolled her eyes. "I never lose."

"Bold words, Mary Margaret. Care to stake some money on that?"

"And how would we judge if I won?"

"I'll be the judge," the Baron chimed in.

"There you go," I told her. "As impartial as they get."

Finally, she just smiled and laughed. "And what would you like, Silas? Half my kingdom?"

"No. How about the price of a boat ticket?"

She stiffened, and I knew that she understood exactly what I meant.

"If I win, if you still can't keep control of tonight, then you run away with me. Anywhere, France or America or Italy...I don't care where. As long as we're together."

She bit her lip. "And if I win?"

"I'll disappear. And leave you to your company and Hugh in peace."

It was a risky gamble—for both of us. If she agreed, she could lose her company. Or I could lose her. Of course, we both knew it was only a game, that I would never press her to leave her company behind if she didn't want to. But either she felt supremely confident in her ability to dominate me or she secretly wanted to lose, because she looked at me and said simply, "Okay."

CHAPTER 12

MOLLY

"Good," Silas said in a husky voice. "Let's get started."

God, looking at him like this—tied up, being serviced, his face full of frustrated lust and suppressed pleasure as he tried to fight off how good Viola was making him feel—I was wet just watching him. Did he really think he could top me from the bottom? Without being able to touch me? When I loved this so much, having him tied up and completely at my disposal to play with as I pleased?

And how much did he really think he had changed? I knew Silas, and Silas had never been the type to turn down sex when it was offered, and even though I now believed he really did love me, I also believed that he was a man through and through, and would be easy enough to tame. Like a cat with cream or a dog with a bone from the kitchen, I would tame him with Viola's pussy.

"Look at this, Silas," I purred, nudging Viola's legs farther apart so that he could see how wet she was, just from playing with his cock. I'd chosen Viola mostly because she looked like me, but also because, despite her somewhat prudish upbringing in an austere town up north, she was a purely sexual creature, the kind whose arousal was uncomplicated and universal. She didn't need to be in control and she didn't need to have control taken from her, she didn't need to be with a man or a woman—all she needed was sex, in any configuration. And Silas was a hell of a configuration; I couldn't blame her for responding to his long, muscled form, stretched into tense and powerful lines.

Silas glanced over to Viola—*victory, he listened to me!*—and then glanced away, looking bored. *Shit.*

"I want to see yours," he said. I don't know how he did it, managing to sound growling and commanding and yet so cultivated at the same time, but however he did it, it sent chills down my spine, and I found myself obeying despite my earlier intention not to, climbing up on the bed and rising up on my knees. *It will tease him more if you show him*, I rationalized. It would rile him up, crack that veneer, and then I would win.

It's just a game, I thought, *a silly dare. It's meaningless.*

But it wasn't meaningless, not really. It didn't matter that the real world stakes might not apply when the sun came up, what mattered were the stakes *now*. Here, in this room, it *was* real. It *did* have meaning, and Silas was right—I had tied him up because I'd known that if I came to him and confessed my own feelings, told him the impact his confession had on me, then he would have laid such a devastatingly complete claim to me that nothing else would have mattered. I would have walked out of this room and surrendered my company happily, I would have said *yes* to Silas's proposal, I would have given up everything because I would belong to Silas and not to myself.

I wasn't ready for that.

Maybe I'd never be ready.

Except I wanted to be, deep down. Wasn't that why I'd agreed to his silly dare? Because part of me wanted him to rise up and claim me, to take care of me—not with money or a house or a legitimate marriage even, but take care of *me*, my inner soul, my inner Mary Margaret O'Flaherty. I wanted there to be one place in my life where I didn't have to be strong, one place where I was able to *rest*.

I spread my legs for Silas.

"You're wet," he rasped. I sensed his desire—his weakness—and decided to exploit it, grabbing Viola by the hips. Silas's cock slid from her mouth with a wet *pop*, and she rose up, her face flushed and her lips swollen and pink from sucking Silas. I kissed those lips, softer and silkier than a man's, and I reached up to stroke her breasts.

Silas did not bother to hide his interest.

Viola and I were on the same side of the bed, and it was easy for me to bend my head down and suckle her breasts. I fluttered my tongue against her nipple, and she arched her back, giving a little cry.

"So you can touch her?" Silas asked. "She can touch you?"

I straightened and pulled Viola in for a close embrace, pressing our bare stomachs together, squeezing our breasts against one another's. Silas's expression didn't change, but out of the corner of my eye, I saw his rigid cock give a surge. He liked seeing Viola and me together. I noted that.

"The contract only says I can't be touched by a man," I clarified. It was a ridiculous oversight. But I supposed those were the narrow-minded men of England for you, even in our modern, industrial times. "I don't think Hugh's solicitors know our habits very well."

Castor laughed from his chair. When I looked over to smile at him, I saw that he was rubbing himself through his trousers, and that sent a bolt of lust through me. Castor was a very experienced and particular man about his tastes—if something aroused him, it had to be quite arousing indeed, and though he wasn't my lover now and would never be again, it still made my core clench thinking that I could affect him like that.

Silas is ridiculous. Obviously, I was born to be in control, and obviously, I was born to love it.

"Viola," Silas said. "I want you to kiss your way down to Molly's breasts right now. Yes, there you go…take one in your hand and then kiss over to her nipple, but don't take it in your mouth."

I sighed at Viola's touch as she obeyed without hesitation, her lips soft and light around my areola.

"Now," Silas said, "put your mouth over her nipple and suck it onto your tongue."

She did, and I nearly moaned out loud from the sensation. I hadn't had someone lavishing attention on my breasts in so very, very long, and Viola seemed keen to make up for all the time I'd lost, her hands braced on my waist as she leaned over and worked me with an eagerness that made Silas clench his jaw.

"That's right," he said. "Now flick your tongue across the tip. Good. Oh, very good—do you feel her waist squirming between your hands? That means you're doing a very good job, Viola. A *very* good job."

Suddenly, I felt a little jealous. I wanted his praise, I wanted to please him, I wanted to be doing a *good job*, because that meant I was a good girl. His good girl.

His Molly.

I reached down and found Viola's cunt with my fingers and began stroking the tight little bud there, looking over at Silas just in time to see his eyes darken and his hands pull unconsciously at his ties.

But fuck, somehow I'd slid out of control, letting him dictate the scene, letting my need to please him override my need to dominate his pleasure. No—it was time for me to take the reins back.

I moved my fingers lower and found Viola even wetter than before. Good.

"I want you to straddle him," I commanded. "And then rub yourself against his dick."

Silas squirmed, either in annoyance or anticipation, straining again at his ties, but the moment Viola's wet pussy started grinding against him, a shudder wracked through his body. I bent down, so my lips were at his ear. "It's going to feel so good when she lets you inside, Silas. It's going to be so tight. So warm. I'm going to make her use you, did you know that? She's going to use that big cock to come and not care how it feels for you, and you are going to feel every pulse and squeeze of it."

"I would rather have it be yours," Silas said, turning his head so that our noses touched. His eyes burned into mine. "I would rather be feeling every pulse and squeeze of my Molly."

Behind me, Viola was rubbing herself eagerly on Silas, the dark head of his cock disappearing and reappearing as she slid herself against it. Her hands were braced on his stomach, her fingernails digging into the firm flesh there. Her head was thrown back, eyes closed, and I knew she would come soon.

Good.

"Viola," I said, rising up to my knees next to her. She stopped moving and looked at me expectantly, her nipples hard and her breathing fast. "Lift up a little. Don't move unless I tell you."

She did, and the moment I reached under her to take Silas's cock in my hand, he groaned, bucking up against his ties and shoving himself deeper into my fist.

I froze. I had only meant to guide him inside of Viola, but his desperate noises with my hand on him, the way his thick length slid through my fist...

Castor cleared his throat, a warning to me that I was getting close to the bounds of the legally forbidden, and I quickly notched the head of Silas's cock against Viola's hole and let go. Now it was Silas that was frozen, sweat starting to gleam on his chest, refusing to move himself upward into Viola's pussy.

That was fine. That was more than fine, actually, because the fact that he wasn't trying to wrest control of the scene away from me meant that he was struggling to keep his wits about him. The bed was wide enough for me to lower myself to my belly and lay my head on Silas's muscled stomach and enjoy the suspended tableau.

Now it was Viola I talked to instead of Silas. "I can see him stretching you," I told her. "Already stretching you and he will stretch you even more when you take him all the way inside." I traced the line where their flesh met with my finger, loving the way I could feel Silas tremble under me. "I can see every vein on Silas. He's so hard right now, so very hard, and all because of you and me. Let's make him feel better, shall we?"

Viola nodded as I knelt once more and took her hips in my hands. And then a small whimper issued from somewhere in her throat as I guided her down, all the way down, impaling her fully on Silas's dick. Silas hissed, every muscle in his thighs and calves looking like carved marble as he kept his body completely still. But he didn't close his eyes, he didn't look away; our stares were locked as I began moving Viola's hips back and forth over him.

"That's it," I whispered to her. "You're doing great."

She whimpered again as I moved her hips faster, forced her to grind harder against him.

"Isn't she doing such a good job, Silas? Isn't her pussy so soft? So wet?"

His jaw tightened.

"It's so fun to move her on you," I continued. "Like she's a plaything that I'm using to fuck you. Like she's a toy, and we're both using her."

"Jesus, Molly," Silas groaned, and finally his eyes squeezed shut, as if he couldn't handle both the sight of me fucking him with Viola's body and my words at the same time.

I bit my lip to hold back my smile. I was winning. Viola would orgasm, and then so would Silas, and I would have won. And more importantly, I would have gotten what I came here for tonight—the chance to give Silas something back. To give him something to hold on to as our paths irrevocably veered off in different directions.

"Use him to come," I commanded Viola. "Ride him as hard as you need."

I let go of her hips as she lost herself on him, squirming and moving up and down, and I dropped my hands down to play with myself, not shocked to find that I was very wet, not shocked to find that my clit was swollen and needy. It wouldn't take long for me to come. And seeing Silas like this...perhaps it was a defect in my personality that I found this sight so delicious, despite what had happened with Mercy. Perhaps I should be jealous that even now he was starting to lose himself in the tight, frantic clench of Viola's cunt, starting to fuck her from the bottom. But the jabbing motion of that thick cock and his narrow hips only served to turn me on more, the sight of him sheathing himself over and over again in Viola just making me greedier for my own climax.

I was too far gone in the scene to care, but I knew I would feel the same way once I was out of it too—that somehow, for Silas and me, this was okay. This wasn't him with Mercy, chasing his own selfish fears. This was he and I *together*, with someone else, and there was nothing but pleasure and happiness here. Even Castor was openly stroking himself now, his eyes hungry on the gasping woman astride Silas.

"Tell me what he feels like," I told Viola, and my voice came out not as authoritative, but rather filled with longing and thirst, and Silas seemed to notice, his eyes opening again and dropping to where my fingers were buried in my own cunt.

"He feels..." Viola took in a deep breath as she continued to work him with frenzied movements of her hips. "He's so big. And *deep*. And *oh...oh God*." The climax took her fast and hard, and she wailed, curling over Silas's chest, her legs instinctively trying to close together, despite still being astride Silas's hips.

The three of us watched her as she slowly came down, slumped against Silas, every curve and rise of her body marked with satiety and contentment. The problem being that the rest of us were nowhere near satisfied and content; Silas looked like a man on a medieval torture rack, every limb and muscle completely tense as Viola still spasmed around his cock, Castor still languidly stroked himself, and I was less rubbing myself now than fucking my own hand.

"Sit up," I demanded to Viola, and she did, slowly, her lids heavy and her face flushed. Once she sat up straight, I moved and swung my leg over Silas, so that I straddled his torso in front of Viola, and so even though it was Viola's pussy still wrapped around his length, it was me that he saw when he looked up.

"Oh my God," he groaned, once he realized what I was doing.

"Now," I said over my shoulder to Viola, "I want you to hold still and let him fuck you. And then I want you to whisper every word that goes through your mind when he does."

And so, with Viola's chest pressed against my back and her arms wrapped tightly around my waist, I began to work my clit as Silas slowly fucked her with long, undulating motions.

Silas's eyes met mine, blue on blue, and I watched every flicker of sensation as it passed across that square-jawed, patrician-bred face of his.

"Ah," Viola breathed into my ear. "He's so big. I feel... stretched. Filled."

Filled. I licked my lips—that word and Silas's mouth opening to whisper my name and his hard stomach bunching and flexing underneath me...all of it sending me closer to the edge.

"I—he's hitting that spot right now." Her voice sounded pained, brittle with pleasure. "The spot on the front. Oh God."

I knew exactly what spot she meant; Silas was one of the only men I'd been with—aside from Castor and Julian—who'd known how to find that spot.

Every.

Single.

Time.

My core clamped in memory, and I slid my fingers down from my clit to my entrance, reaching up inside to curl my fingers to where I wanted Silas's cock.

And then he started talking, hoarse and demanding. "I can

feel how wet you are, Mary Margaret. You're wet all over my stomach, and I can feel how slippery your fingers are from fucking your own pussy." Silas stabbed his hips up and Viola cried out.

"So deep," she gasped into my ear. "I can feel him every-where...my hips feel so tight and my thighs are tight too and it's so hard to breathe...shit, I'm going to come again."

"Not yet," Silas growled. "Viola, I want you to take those hands that you have so prettily wrapped around my Molly's waist, and I want you to move them down to Molly's cunt. Yes, just like that. And now take one and push it inside of her, and then use the other to work her clit. Molly, I want you to take *your* fingers and press them against my mouth so I can taste you."

He's trying to take over again, I realized, but at that moment, his tongue danced across the already-wet pads of my fingertips and Viola found the right pressure and pace, and I didn't care.

"Viola," Silas said, his breath tickling against my fingers, "you can't come until Molly comes. Do you understand?"

"Yes, Silas," she breathed against my shoulder, resting her forehead there as Silas began fucking her from below. Her fingers were magic, but even more magic was Silas underneath us, all muscles and man and need, covered with sweat, his face angry and worshipful all at once as he sucked on my fingers and drove his cock into Viola.

I pulled my fingers back to knead my breast, and he started saying words, filthy words that were so wrong and so raw, words that stroked the inside of me like I wanted his cock to. *Do you like another girl in your pussy?* and *she feels so good, Molly, you picked a good one* and *sit on my face, God, I'd kill someone to have you on my face right now.*

I knew what Viola meant about everything being tight—my neck and back and stomach and even my feet felt ready to snap, ready to shatter like so much glass, and it felt like there was nothing but those fingers on my cunt and Silas's beautiful eyes and filthy mouth.

"I'm going to fuck her pussy like it's yours," he said to me, only to me, as if we were the only people really here. "I'm going to make her take my cock, and you're going to feel every minute of it and know that each and every stroke is for you. And you are going to look me in the eyes while you come and it will be my name you scream. Understood?"

"Y-yes," I shivered out; Viola's were fingers so good and so strong and so fast. "Yes."

"Please," Viola begged in my ear. "Please hurry. I can't wait much longer—"

Her voice broke off as Silas thrust upward at double the pace, a delighted laugh bursting from him as he watched both Viola and I tumble over the cliff and plunge to the rocks below.

She went first, and it was her hitched gasp, her fingers digging into me as her body was taken, that triggered my own release. I went hot, then cold, feverish and fervent and almost hallucinatory as my world shrank down to his grin and his eyes blazing blue with victory and our little pleasure doll behind me, barely holding on for dear life as she convulsed through her second orgasm of the night.

"*Silas,*" I breathed, the word catching in my throat.

The waves started deep in my center, but quickly exploded outward, my toes curling as every muscle rippled with release and a deep and primal satisfaction, and I could barely breathe, the entirety of the erotic scene driving my orgasm on and on and on until I was slumped back against Viola, my head leaning back to rest on her shoulder.

"Jesus Christ," Silas said, a little desperately, as both of us girls gradually finished climaxing on top of him. "Jesus fucking Christ."

Viola gave a tired little laugh from behind me.

Silas's voice was rough and brooked no argument when he said, "Untie me right the fuck now."

I should have said no. This was definitely me losing our little bet, but I couldn't deny it any longer. Silas was what I wanted. Silas *dominating* me was what I wanted. And when he murmured, "That's my good Molly," when I slid off the bed and went to the bottom posts to unknot his feet, I felt a flush of pleasure that I would have given anything to feel all the time. A flush that told me that I was his, that I was taken care of, that when I was with him, I could relax and feel safe.

As I worked on the knot by Silas's ankle, Castor came up to me. "Are you finished with Viola?" he asked quietly.

I glanced up to Silas. The look on his face told me that whatever was going to happen next was going to happen between him and me alone. "Yes," I replied.

"Then I'm taking her, if she agrees. Can I trust you two to behave yourselves? I'd rather not commit perjury if I can help it, but…" He trailed off, his face hard as he looked at Viola's naked form, which was currently curled into a ball of pale limbs and red hair. His erection bulged under the trousers that he hadn't bother to button when he'd pulled them back up.

"I understand, believe me."

He nodded curtly and walked over to Viola, where he gently swept the hair from her face. "Would you like to go to bed with me?" he asked.

She made a purring noise of assent, and he gathered her into his arms, and then they were gone. I turned my attention back to Silas; with one leg freed, I moved to the other, admiring the long, strong bands of muscle that made up his calves and thighs and stomach and chest.

His erection had not abated—if anything, it had grown harder, the head a dark purple, and the shaft so rigid that it didn't lay flat against his stomach; instead it pulsed with every beat of his heart, the pre-cum beading at the tip betraying exactly how aroused he was.

He didn't say anything as I moved up to his right hand, and the lack of chatter from him made me nervous. Silas was a talker, a charmer, the kind of person you could count on to fill any awkward gaps in conversation with easy, polite chatter and an infectious laugh. But not right now. Right now, he watched me in silence, a silence that wasn't stern or solemn necessarily, but a silence that was practically electrified with power.

Castor and I had tied the knots well, but we hadn't made them very tight since we hadn't wanted to wake Silas as we worked. But Silas's thrashing and straining had yanked the silk ties fast, especially around his wrists. It took me a few minutes to pull apart the first one, and even longer for the second, and still he didn't speak, his eyes pinned on me the entire time.

But the moment I finally pulled the last knot loose, he was on me, his hands on my throat and waist, and then I was on my back, his knees on either side of my shoulders, his large hand gripping my jaw and forcing my head to tilt back.

"I won't violate your fucking contract," he said, and I didn't need to see to know that his other hand fisted his dick. "But you're going to take this, every drop of it, for making me fuck someone else. For teasing me. For walking away on the ball-room floor tonight."

Earlier, I would have fought him. I would have teased him or provoked him, but not now. I wanted to be under him, subsumed by him, humiliated by him. Everything about it felt so *right* and I would never feel this way again and *oh my God*...I would never feel this way again. How could I live like that? Without Silas?

I'd asked myself that question so many times in the last week, but now, with him clutching my jaw, ready to ejaculate all over me, I realized how terrible it all was. I belonged here, under-neath him, covered in him, and I would be lost without this.

He relaxed his grip just enough so that I could see the glorious sight of him stroking his cock. "My Molly," he breathed as he tightened his fist. "My Mary Margaret."

"Say it again," I begged.

It became a prayer on his lips, a chant of power and owner-ship. "My Molly. My Molly. My M—*fuck!*"

His stomach muscles seized and jerked, tightening into deli-ciously tight lines, and his thighs clenched, and then he finally gave it all up to me, ropes of semen on my face and neck and hair, hot pulses of cum as he growled my name over and over, *Molly Molly, my Molly*, fucking his fist through it all, as if to milk himself for every drop. And the whole time, he'd kept those strong fingers wrapped around my jaw, holding me still as he marked me. As he claimed me in the basest way possible.

He didn't let go of my jaw right away, and neither did the lust fade from his eyes. Instead, he examined every inch of my face with a possessive satisfaction, as if seeing me covered in his cum answered some deep, existential question for him.

I let my tongue move slowly, licking him off my lips as he watched.

He grunted and released my face. "You're mine now."

My eyelids burned at this. Why had I been so stupidly blind and proud last year? Yes, he'd fucked up, but now I'd broken our future as well. If instead of punching him and letting him leave, I had instead punched him and then forced him to make it up to me…we could be married now. We could have a *forever* together.

"I'm yours," I whispered.

"And I won," he declared with no small amount of satisfac-tion. Despite letting go of my face, he kept me pinned to the bed, his knees still astride my shoulders. And I loved it. He had won, and I welcomed the reminder, the reminder that I belonged to him. I would pretend that right now was for forever, that I had thousands of nights of him claiming me to look forward to.

I would pretend that this wasn't both the first and last time that he would get to own me.

"You did win," I said, my voice choked with the knowledge that this was almost at an end. *No, Molly. Pretend, pretend, pretend, just for now. Just for tonight.*

He trailed a long finger down my neck, running it through

his essence, his half-hard cock stiffening as he reviewed the evidence of my submission. And then, with a reluctant growl, Silas moved off of me and went over to the table at the edge of the room. He returned with a damp towel and cleaned my face and neck and hair, saying nothing, although the low rumbles of satisfaction vibrating through his chest told me everything I needed to know.

After he finished, he tossed the towel to the side and reclined against the pillows at the top of the bed, crushing me to his chest as he did. I rarely felt this slender, this small, this *female*...but gathered in Silas's arms and pressed against his firm chest, I decided that I could get used to it.

"So where are we going?" he asked.

"Pardon?" I murmured.

"I won, remember? And we're going to run away together. Where shall we go? France? Belgium? I hear New York City is quite exciting."

Pretend, pretend. Pretend that it's not just more London and more misery and more Hugh awaiting you in the morning.

I shook my head. "Ireland. We're going to Ireland."

"Of course. To Ennis, I suppose?"

I closed my eyes, loving the feeling of his heart beating deep within his chest, a heart that I knew was mine for the taking.

Pretend.

"For a while," I answered him, eyes still closed, allowing the scene to play out in my mind. "And then we'd go to a house on the coast."

"Sounds wet," Silas spoke into my hair, playfulness creeping back into his tone. "But I like it when things are...wet."

"You are so much less clever than you think you are."

"Then it's a good thing I have you around to remind me. So what would our lives be like on this Irish coast? Would you try to make a fisherman out of me?"

I smiled at the image of my urbane, sophisticated Silas trying to fish. "No, we'd simply live our lives. Take walks, read books, make love."

"Get married," he added.

"In my childhood church," I said. "You'll have to become Catholic."

"A papist? Only for you. I imagine all of our children would be little papist heathens as well?" His hands slid down to lace together over my stomach.

Pretend pretend. "Yes," I said, and I was glad he couldn't see my face and how close I was to crying. "All of our blue-eyed children."

He slid deeper into the pillows, taking me with him, until we were snuggled so perfectly that I wanted to die here so that I would never have to leave. "I love you, Mary Margaret," he said in a sleepy voice.

"I love you too," I managed, hoping that he wouldn't feel the way my ribs threatened to jerk and twitch with suppressed sobs.

"And tomorrow," he said, words thick with doziness. "Tomorrow we sail for Ireland."

"Yes." I whispered the lie into his skin. "Tomorrow."

Silas and Molly aren't finished with each other yet...

Find out what happens next in the conclusion to their story,
The Wedding of Molly O'Flaherty!

Keep reading to learn more!

READY TO FIND OUT WHAT
HAPPENS WITH MOLLY AND SILAS?

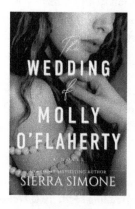

One empty bed.
One bold plan.
One tragedy that changes everything.

***

Silas Cecil-Coke is not a man who is easily dissuaded. So when
Molly leaves his bed without a word of goodbye, he is even more
determined to save her from her enemies and claim her as his
bride.

159

But neither of them are prepared for the betrayals and tragedies that await them before they can even approach the altar...

~

I was **so excited** to be back in Sierra Simone's **decadent world of lust, love, and money**. Simone has once again proven why historical romances are her forte. " --**The Fairest of All Book Reviews**

"**HOT D*MN, but Silas is HOT**! I love his **playful, charming, happy** side, but oh my gosh, I love his **deliciously dominant, possessive** side even more! He's just totally **shiver and swoon-worthy**, not to mention that he'll make a lot more than just your heart melt. **Silas is an awesome, protective, and dedicated hero** and I absolutely loooooved him!!" --**A Hopeless Romantic's Booklandia**

"Oh, unf. I have **loved every word** of The London Lovers. Silas and Molly were such a fantastic match and they **flew off the page** with Sierra Simone's **talented and passionate** mind." --**Melanie Martin**

Read the steamy conclusion to Silas and Molly's story now in *The Wedding of Molly O'Flaherty!*

ALSO BY SIERRA SIMONE

Thornchapel:

A Lesson in Thorns

Feast of Sparks

Harvest of Sighs

Door of Bruises

Misadventures:

Misadventures with a Professor

Misadventures of a Curvy Girl

Misadventures in Blue

The New Camelot Trilogy:

American Queen

American Prince

American King

The Moon (Merlin's Novella)

American Squire (A Thornchapel and New Camelot Crossover)

The Priest Series:

Priest

Midnight Mass: A Priest Novella

Sinner

Saint (coming early fall 2021)

Co-Written with Laurelin Paige

Porn Star

Hot Cop

The Markham Hall Series:

The Awakening of Ivy Leavold

The Education of Ivy Leavold

The Punishment of Ivy Leavold (now including the novella *The Reclaiming of Ivy Leavold*)

The London Lovers:

The Seduction of Molly O'Flaherty (now bundled with the novella *The Persuasion of Molly O'Flaherty*)

The Wedding of Molly O'Flaherty

ACKNOWLEDGMENTS

My women: Laurelin Paige, Kayti McGee, Melanie Harlow, Geneva Lee, and Tamara Mataya. Thank you to Nancy Smay of Evident Ink for your amazing edits, and Cait, my patient forbearing formatter. To Linda, Sarah and Candi, who make sure I can hide in my cave.

To my Dirty Laundry Girls and the Literary Gossip Girls. Your support is amazing. To all the other blogs that have been so kind to Sierra Simone—TRSOR, Natasha's A Book Junkie, Shh Mom's Reading, Maryse's Book Blog, Schmexy Girl Book Blog, True Story Book Blog, Fiction Fangirls, and so many others that I know I'm forgetting. THANK YOU!

ABOUT THE AUTHOR

Sierra Simone is a USA Today bestselling former librarian who spent too much time reading romance novels at the information desk. She lives with her husband and family in Kansas City.

Sign up for her newsletter to be notified of releases, books going on sale, events, and other news!

www.thesierrasimone.com
thesierrasimone@gmail.com

CPSIA information can be obtained
at www.ICGtesting.com
Printed in the USA
FSHW010640100521
81277FS